THE BIG REVEAL

CRUSHING

JUDE WARNE

EPIC
Escape

An Imprint of EPIC Press
EPICPRESS.COM

The Big Reveal
Crushing: Book #3

Written by Jude Warne

Copyright © 2018 by Abdo Consulting Group, Inc.

Published by EPIC Press™
PO Box 398166
Minneapolis, MN 55439

All rights reserved.

Printed in the United States of America.

Cover design by Laura Mitchell
Images for cover art obtained from iStockPhoto.com
Edited by K. A. Rue

LIBRARY OF CONGRESS CATALOGING-IN-PUBLICATION DATA
Names: Warne, Jude, author.
Title: The big reveal / by Jude Warne.
Description: Minneapolis, MN : EPIC Press, 2018. | Series: Crushing
Summary: Aspiring actor Blake has just joined the theater troupe at Duncan High. When Blake
    falls hard for his new scene partner, openly gay Dustin, he must reconsider his identity, and
    Blake's mom is less than supportive. Can Blake be true to himself, honest with his mom,
    and open himself up to a real relationship with Dustin?
Identifiers: LCCN 2016962596 | ISBN 9781680767179 (lib. bdg.)
    | ISBN 9781680767735 (ebook)
Subjects: LCSH: High schools—Fiction. | Gay teenagers—Fiction. | Young adult fiction.
Classification: DDC [Fic]—dc23
LC record available at http://lccn.loc.gov/2016962596

For Everyone

Applause. Applause surrounded me. It was just like that dream I kept having, except this time the people applauding were my drama teachers, Mr. Perske and Ms. Miller. In my dream the applauders were usually the top-ranking directors working in Hollywood, plus the ghost of Stanley Kubrick, the best director who had ever lived.

In reality, I had just finished reciting the famous "To be or not to be" monologue from Shakespeare's *Hamlet*. In reality, I had just finished auditioning for my school's best extracurricular—the Theater Troupe. And I had just aced it—at least if I was interpreting Mr. Perske's and Ms. Miller's applause correctly.

I was a sophomore at Duncan High School in Eastport, Maine, the easternmost place in the whole country. East of Eastport was the Atlantic Ocean. My cousin Luisa, who lived in Idaho, always told me how jealous she was that I lived so close to New York City. She wanted to be a singer and I wanted to be an actor and we both wanted to move there. I always reminded her though, that it was a *ten-hour drive* from here to Manhattan. I might as well live in Idaho myself for all the good Eastport did me.

As naturally beautiful as the landscape was, there was nothing current, nothing fashionable, and nothing *that* relevant to modern life in Eastport. It was hard to find places to get artistic kicks from—if a person happened to want those kinds of kicks, which I did. Eastport was made up of Main Street, two or three restaurants, a general store, a florist, a market, and then stretches of blank streets followed by rows of houses. Eastport—the town impossible to get lost in.

Mr. Perske and Ms. Miller tried their best to add creative flair to Duncan High, and I loved them for that. They were both English teachers who had started up an afterschool Theater Troupe last spring; I hadn't been able to join then because I had only been a freshman. To be part of the troupe, a student had to be a sophomore or older. I had waited all summer for my chance and September had finally come.

At the moment, it was a Wednesday afternoon during the second week of classes.

"Bravo, Blake!" Ms. Miller exclaimed. My name even sounded like an actor's name.

"Excellent read, Blake. Quite inspired. You'll be hearing from us very soon," Mr. Perske added. "The results of Troupe tryouts will be posted on the Activities bulletin board by next week."

I hoped he was telling the truth this time, only

because announcements from the Theater Troupe were notoriously posted late at Duncan High.

"Next week?" I repeated, to draw attention to Mr. Perske's promise. I picked up my backpack from its spot in the corner of the classroom and placed it carefully on my back. The reflection in the plate glass window proved that I looked stellar—shiny jet black hair cut in a fashionable James Dean style, impeccable white V-neck, dark blue Levis, and my best combat boots. *I* would hire me as an actor, and *I* would definitely admit me into the Theater Troupe, if I were Mr. Perske and Ms. Miller.

At least, I was pretty *sure* I would. I tried to be optimistic in the face of uncertainty.

Moving toward the door, I flashed a big smile.

"By the end of next week, yes," Mr. Perske confirmed. "In the meantime, keep practicing that monologue. Watch the Ethan Hawke version of *Hamlet* over the weekend. Set in modern times and very relatable. It'll help you get into character."

I was pretty sure that Vera had this on DVD, because her collection was awesome. She had good taste in pretty much everything. Vera was my mom, and I had called her Vera since I was a tiny kid—she even encouraged it. She was the coolest mom who had ever existed, and she stuck out like a sore thumb in Eastport.

As I left Mr. Perske and Ms. Miller, I remembered how far from Broadway or Hollywood I actually was, logistically speaking. Eastport got its name from fact. We were the first ones in the country to see the sun rise every morning . . . if someone was enough of a nerd to get up that early. Which I *of course* was not, and neither was Vera.

Vera always said that she did everything she could to get away from Brunswick, Maine, which was where she went to high school. She once rode a Greyhound bus all the way to Concord, New Hampshire—en route to New York City—before she was found out by the bus driver, who had been clued in to a missing sixteen-year-old on the run. Vera had wanted to be a fashion model in her day, and by the looks of the old Polaroids I'd found around our house, she could have been one. She was tall with a charismatic smile and glittering green eyes. If I'd been a casting agent then, I would've signed her. I've seen tons of movies and I know what success looks like. I know what the people want. At least I think I do.

Vera was sent back to her parents amidst her runaway stint then, but she managed to hit up SUNY Purchase for college down the line and majored in Drama. She moved to New York City when she graduated to look for an agent, or an understudy gig in an off-Broadway play, or an extra part on a film. Vera waitressed in a diner a few afternoons a week then, which is where she met the sculptor, my dad Bobby, who was a regular customer there. Fell in love, moved out to Eastport where Bobby was from, got married, had me, fourteen years went by, got divorced. Then Bobby left us flat and moved back to New York City. I hadn't seen my dad in thirteen months. And I really, honestly, did not care.

But I didn't want to think about that whole mess at the moment. I wanted to ride the high from my Troupe audition for as long as I could.

I unchained my bike from its spot on the rack outside Duncan High, eyeing the pines in the near distance whose green needles were blowing in the impatient wind. It seemed to be a good omen that things would be moving ahead in the best possible way. I had been working on the *Hamlet* monologue all through August, so I hoped it was true.

Bravo, Blake! Ms. Miller had said. *Quite inspired,* Mr. Perske had said. Duncan's Drama Troupe was a highly-coveted group to be a part of in Eastport; entry guaranteed a student membership until graduation.

I let go of my bike's brake and sped down the long hill that connected Duncan to the Main Street in Eastport. The mild September breeze blew in off the water and from the pines in the distance. As I passed by the town square, I saw the four o'clock Greyhound pulling out of its stop and heading east toward New York. I tried to imagine Vera boarding a Greyhound years ago from her town, with just one suitcase and her battered collection of Tennessee Williams plays. We still had the book at home, and every once in a while I would take it down from its spot on the shelf and do some scene work.

Our place was only about a mile from school. We lived in a very small white house on a spare bit of street with only a few other houses on it. The house was kind of like a seaside cottage with small rooms—just one floor, and then a half-floor—a loft—where I slept. From my window, if I stood on one foot and leaned forward as far as possible, I could see the ocean way far off. It was beautiful, always. But sometimes, especially after watching a movie that took place in New York or that was filmed in a Hollywood studio, looking at the sea and cliffs made me feel stranded. Like there was nowhere to go, no matter how much I wanted to. Like I would have to stay right where I was no matter what.

"Vera!" I yelled as I burst through the front door into our living room.

There was no response. I looked at the clock on the wall to see that it was four-fifteen p.m.; Vera meditated every day at four o'clock. If we were out shopping, if we had guests over, she would excuse herself and go to a private space, whether it was her bedroom or the car in the mall parking lot. She called it the best compulsion she ever had and insisted that it was the reason for her sanity, especially since Dad left. Especially since Dad had met Audrey.

Audrey was the woman with whom Dad lived now in New York. I had only met her once, when she and Dad stopped here on the way back from visiting my grandparents at their retirement home in Augusta last year. She was young, overly nice, and had a soft and sultry voice. I couldn't stand her. Why Dad chose to move in with her instead of living with us, rather than be with cooler-than-cool Vera, I would never understand. Didn't he care about our family at all? Besides, he and Vera used to be best friends. I kept reminding myself that I didn't care about seeing Dad anymore.

Something had happened when he started spending more time in New York for his adjunct teaching job with the School of Visual Arts. Since I was a baby, Dad had worked on his sculptures and taught Art at Duncan Middle School. Every few months he'd have a showing at Eastport's one art gallery, The Show Room. But then out of the blue his old mentor called him up on the phone—this guru guy from Brooklyn, Elia Rumpelmeyer. He had supervised Dad's college thesis a million years ago, so he offered this once-a-week gig to Dad at his alma mater, teaching Sculpting Craft to freshmen at SVA. He still kept his middle school job, but every Thursday morning he'd fly down to New York, teach the class that night, and fly back the next morning to teach his afternoon art classes at Duncan. Vera had said it was a temporary thing.

This was the one and only time that Vera had been wrong.

After a month of the new setup, Dad took to spending his entire weekends in New York, coming home late on Sunday nights after I was already in bed. I'd wake up to find him asleep on our couch, with Vera tight-lipped, frying eggs in the kitchen. I'd remember hearing raised voices from the night before. I knew then that something was going on.

I'd always been closer with Vera, because while Dad would spend hours working on his pieces in our basement studio, Vera would spend time with me. She helped me with my homework, made us awesome meals, and took me to see every movie that ever passed through the Eastport Theater. When I reached middle school, she'd come home every Friday with a new play for me to read and study and practice my acting with. We bonded over our mutual love of the theater. Vera could charm the pants off of anybody but Dad was different. He was quiet, thoughtful, and sometimes stormy. You could never tell what he was thinking.

Then one Sunday Dad just didn't come home. That was two years ago. When I asked Vera where he was, she just said that SVA had assigned him extra classes for the week. But the week came and went and Dad had still not come back. When I texted him, he told me that he was fine and that he missed me, but that I should ask Vera for details.

The details spelled separation, which apparently had a whole lot to do with this woman, Audrey. A month later Dad came back to move all of his stuff out, saying that he was renting a studio in the East Village of Manhattan, and that in the fall, he would take over from Elia the Head-of-Program title at SVA.

Right after that, Vera took to spending nearly all of her time at the Eastport Bookstore where she worked. It snowed like crazy that December, and sometimes it would be nearly ten o'clock on a Tuesday night, with me just finishing up my Global Studies essay, and Vera still not home. I would throw on my snow boots, parka, wool hat, the works to trudge my bike through the snow and go check on her. Whenever I called her cellphone she never answered, always forgetting to leave it on. Half an hour later I'd arrive to find her at the main counter, with Frank Sinatra's saddest album playing on the store's Spotify account. She was reorganizing the entire store, switching entire genre sections all on her own and re-wallpapering the walls.

I'd knock three times on the windowpane to let her know I was there. She'd look up and motion that she was coming. Ten minutes later she'd lock up the store and we'd walk back home together in silence through the relentless snow. We never said a word to each other then.

But Vera was strong and that period in our lives had only lasted three months or so. Now she was completely back to normal—she had told me several times. She was over Dad, she said.

I threw myself down on the couch and ran through my *Hamlet* monologue again; it sounded almost as good as it had during the audition. I couldn't wait to find out whether I had made it into Duncan's Theater Troupe or not. It would be great experience and would look good on my college application in a few years. I wanted to study Drama at Juilliard. I wanted to live and work in New York City.

I reached for my Android in my back pocket to see what was going on, if anything. There was a text from Ming Xia, my best friend. Ming was a sophomore at Duncan too, and she loved to paint these crazy images on manuscript paper with watercolors. She called them dreamscape paintings. We planned on moving to New York together for college, with me at Juilliard and her at School of Visual Arts where Dad worked.

How'd it go, Blake? Did your Hamlet wow Perske and Miller??!!

I smiled to myself as I texted back Of course I did. Don't you know me at all?

Ming was the fastest texter I had ever met. Good to know your humility's still intact ;). Proud of you, Blake. Are you ready for our filming soon?

I had totally forgotten! Yes, of course I was ready. I had been born ready! Ming had come up with the idea to drum up some publicity for my career as an actor by posting my monologue readings on YouTube for the world of the internet to see. If we got a following of viewers going, who knew what could happen. Maybe a casting agent would see it and ask me to fly out to Los Angeles— start out small, with television commercials, then soap operas, then with feature films that generated plenty of Oscar buzz. Anything was possible. The internet was a magical place.

Thanks ☺ Readier than ever, Ming.

"Blake honey, is that you?"

I looked up from my Android as Vera emerged

from her meditation session. She looked refreshed and happy, her long black hair hanging loose down her back.

"Yeah, Vera, it's me. Home from school."

She widened her eyes more and took a deep breath, getting re-accustomed to the light and to reality. Sometimes her meditations got really intense—she'd see visions of people she said she'd been in past lives. When you hear stuff like that it makes you never want to meditate ever.

"So?" Vera prompted, proceeding to wash kale and romaine leaves that had been out on the counter.

"So what?" I joked back.

"Blake," more annoyed this time, "how did it go? The audition?"

I put some ice in two glasses and poured some sparkling water out for us. "Oh, yeah," I replied, purposely slow. "The audition."

Vera rolled her eyes as she chopped up tomatoes and cucumbers. "Well—did Mr. Perske and Ms.

Miller say anything? Were you happy with it, more importantly?"

I held my tongue. I loved to tease Vera like this because she cared so much about me. She didn't have the patience to tease back.

She heaved a dramatic sigh and took a drink from her water glass, hand on one hip. She gave me that look, the one that let me know to cut it out.

"Yeah, Mr. Perske said something, what was it . . . oh yeah, he threw out some words . . . 'excellent . . . quite inspired . . . you'll be hearing from us very soon,' I think they were."

Vera's face lit up and she threw her arms around me in a bear hug.

"Blake, I'm so proud of you! That's fantastic! Didn't I tell you your reading was amazing?"

I had practiced my monologue for Vera and Ming last night, and they had given it a standing O.

"Dad will be proud too—you missed his call earlier but I told him you'd call him back tonight."

I suddenly felt agitated and annoyed.

"Oh yeah?" I replied.

"Blake, you're going to have to talk to him sooner or later. He's your father and he loves you."

I wasn't so sure about that.

"**B**lake, you have *got* to calm down. There's this entire class to get through before we can go and check the Activities bulletin board. Would you try and stay still, at least?"

Ming and I sat at our desks in the Global Studies room, in my last scheduled class of the day. It was Wednesday, and Mr. Perske had assured me that same morning when I ran into him in the hall that the Troupe tryout results would be posted at the end of the day. I had been in a cold sweat since then. Part of me was so sure that I'd made it in. The other part of me wasn't.

Ming took out her textbook and notebook and started to copy down the daily aim from the white-board. Mr. Walker, our Global Studies teacher, was starting our section on The Crusades today, which we were scheduled to study for the next three weeks—almost as long as the real Crusades it seemed. I liked Mr. Walker, though. He was the one who first told me about the film *Lion in Winter* starring my favorite actor, or one of them, Peter O' Toole. Mr. Walker liked the movie because of its depiction of British Royal history. It featured King Henry I, his three crazy sons, and his wife Katharine Hepburn—or Eleanor of Aquitaine—whom he kept locked away in a tower. We had watched the movie in class on the first day of the semester.

Mr. Walker came gliding into the classroom as the final bell rang. He was cool—half young, half mature, with long graying hair and always wearing skinny neckties. I wasn't sure whether he knew about the Theater Troupe postings but I hoped he would let us out of class early today.

Right behind Mr. Walker came Kendra Morrison and Zoe Pepper, two nice-enough but slightly brown-nosey girls, with their friend Dustin Dern. I was pretty sure that Dustin had tried out for the Troupe too because I had heard him talking about it to Zoe last week in the hallway.

Dustin shook his shiny blonde curls away from his face as he dramatically took a seat in the front row. I saw Ming give Dustin a quick onceover when he came into the room. Pretty much every girl in Duncan High School, at one time or another, had crushed on Dustin Dern. He looked kind of like a young Leonardo DiCaprio, and he was smart, nice, and as charming as anything. Unfortunately for the female population of Eastport, their attraction to Dustin could never really be returned. Dustin never noticed the girls—not that way.

Dustin was gay. Everyone at Duncan, and pretty much everyone in Eastport, had known it since last semester. Dustin hadn't made a big deal out of it or anything. If I remember correctly, I think he had just told Kendra and Zoe, and then by the end of that day, everyone in Duncan High knew. Not like *that* was a big feat—Duncan didn't have that many students. Eastport was a small place.

To be honest, at the time, nobody was all that surprised to hear the news. Most of us had assumed as much for as long as we could remember, mostly because Dustin never really commented on the attractiveness of girls. He sometimes wore mascara too. Kendra and Zoe would use him as their model during lunch period, testing out different looks on him. He never bothered to take it off afterwards. I always thought makeup looked good on Dustin. But maybe that was the actor in me.

Right after Dad moved away last year—this always sticks out in my mind—one lonely Sunday night I waited for Vera outside of her shop, and Dustin came by. I mean, I don't think he came by on *purpose*, to see me and Vera or anything. I just think he was on his way home from the Eastport movie theater. He saw me standing there in the snow and waved—this is kind of embarrassing actually. I had been crying. Not outright weeping, just a reserved, stalwart, soldier-esque tear-shedding. This was out of character for me, of course. But Vera and I were going through a rough time, not talking all that much, both of us knowing that Dad wasn't coming back.

"What's wrong, Blake?" Dustin had asked, his furrowed eyebrows covered in snowflakes, his right hand on my shoulder. I hadn't spoken to anybody other than Ming about what was going on with Vera and Dad. I looked up into Dustin's eyes. I was shaking from the cold.

"My parents," I said, choking back tears. "They're splitting up. I haven't seen my dad in weeks."

I could hardly see for all the snow and tears. Dustin seemed torn apart, like he had just received the worst news.

"I'm so sorry. That's really rough," he said.

Hearing it said out loud, hearing myself say it out loud as a fact, *my parents, they're splitting up*, made me realize it was true. It was all really happening and it was happening to me. I started bawling.

Dustin wrapped his arms around me in a big bear hug and held me as I cried. The memory of it made me feel a bit embarrassed.

Now, every time I saw him in the hall at school or around Main Street, he always gave me a big hello and I gave him one right back. It was like we had a secret, a bond, an agreement. I couldn't really explain it exactly, but whatever it was, it was nice and I liked it.

Mr. Walker's Crusades lecture was worse than I had thought possible. I tried to translate the information that he was feeding us into dramatic and entertaining scenes in my mind, like the ones in movies, full of blood and guts and honor and treachery and lust and vengeance. Every time I tried, though, my mind wandered back to the memory of my audition with Mr. Perske and Ms. Miller. *You'll be hearing from us very soon.* I hoped so. If this was what being an actor was going to be like—waiting for hours, for days, to hear back about an audition, with no guarantee of a positive outcome—I wasn't so sure.

The minutes dragged by. I took detailed notes while Mr. Walker rambled on in order to distract myself from my anxiety over the Troupe announcement. My hand was nearly numb from writing and I had filled ten pages in my notebook when the last bell of the day rang. Classes were over. The Troupe members list was now posted on the Activities bulletin board.

"Make sure you read chapters four through—" Mr. Walker started to say, but I was already out the door. I would get the assignment from Ming later.

Suddenly it seemed that the halls of Duncan had never been so crowded before. I stepped on the heels of nearly ten different students in an effort to get to the end of the first floor hall where the list would be posted. Finally, after what seemed like forever, I got there.

Blake Teller. First name on the list.

I heard echoes of praise around me: "Good job!" and "Well done," and pats on the back from all. I heard a few groans of disappointment too; Kendra stood a few feet away, her face wearing a pronounced frown.

"I can't say I'm surprised," said Ming, who now stood to my right, holding my Global Studies textbook. "Now we *have* to do the YouTube series."

"Thanks, Ming. Whatever you say." I was elated and didn't feel like arguing with her. Still, I wasn't one hundred percent convinced that the YouTube web series was the best way to go if I wanted to be a serious actor. I wanted to devote myself to the stage before I thought seriously about film. The internet was a couple of steps below film, too. I wanted to be like Laurence Olivier—he had never filmed a YouTube series and he had done just fine.

"You excited, Blake?"

I turned around to see Dustin standing behind me, beaming from ear to ear. It seemed that he had been accepted into the Theater Troupe too.

"Yeah, man, it's gonna be great. What about you?"

He ran his fingers through his hair and made a face like he was lost for words.

"I am indeed. Can't wait to work with you. With everybody," he added hastily. Dustin turned a slight shade of pink and looked away. Suddenly I became very aware of myself—how I was standing, wondering whether Ming or anyone else was watching us. Why should it matter, though? We weren't doing anything wrong.

"Congrats, Blake—to both of us," Dustin clarified, patting me on the back. I felt the heat from his hand, which stayed there a second too long. Was I losing my mind or was something? Was I just imagining this?

Just then Zoe came over and tugged at Dustin's shirtsleeve. She was always chewing gum, her frizzy red hair clipped back against her head with the same deplorably pink barrettes.

"Dusty, will you come over here, please? Kendra is a total wreck. She really thought she was gonna make it in. I told her that this whole thing is no big deal, but she won't listen to me."

As they walked off I felt a strange sensation that I tried to push down to the deepest part of myself. Whatever it was, I didn't want to deal with it right now. Besides, it was distracting me from my victory.

"Celebratory milkshake at Harvey's?" Ming proposed to me, still holding my textbook from earlier. Harvey's was the best, and only, diner in town.

"Sounds like a plan. Then I've got to go home and tell Vera the good news."

———

"Blake Teller, I could not be more proud of you!"

Vera threw her grocery bags down, her jacket

and pocketbook still on, and threw her arms around me when I told her. She had just walked in the door, home from work.

"Thank you so much, Vera. You can let go of me now."

She did and began to unpack the bag of groceries.

"I'm glad that this fantastic purchase was not made in vain. We'll have to have it tonight!"

Vera pulled out a bakery box and opened it to reveal my favorite cake in the entire world from Loretta's Market, Sour Cream Chocolate Chip. My sugar levels were destined to go into overdrive today. First a black-and-white milkshake with Ming, then a few hunks of Loretta's cake. But celebration was in order and this seemed a pretty great way to do it.

"So," Vera said as she served up two slices for us, "how did it happen? How did you hear?"

I stuffed a forkful of cake into my mouth.

"Posted, on the Activities board. Mine was the first name."

"Be careful, Blake. Don't choke. Wow, that's so lovely, honey. Do you know what you'll be working on?"

I thought about it for a moment as I swallowed the cake and reached for some more. I had absolutely no idea.

"I'm not sure, Vera. The whole thing is very mysterious. I think we spend the semester on scene work. And by the end of it, we put on a play."

Once, in eighth grade, I had done a two-week stint at Maine State Youth Arts Camp, during which I played the part of Puck from *Midsummer Night's Dream* for two straight weeks. Total character immersion with a bunch of other twelve-year-olds. It had made its mark on me though, because it had been my first experience of what it could be like to be an actor, to be onstage, to be in the spotlight, to have an audience pay attention to me and only me. To depict a full range of human emotions, the emotions that I felt on a consistent basis throughout my everyday life. I know I had only been a kid at the time, but it was the first time I had really gotten it.

"Well, I can't wait to see you onstage," Vera concluded. Neither could I.

"Raise your arms up, two, three, bring your arms down, two, three. Breathe altogether now, breathe as one group," Ms. Miller said. She was playing sitar music on the busted-up boom box that belonged to the Duncan faculty. The fourteen of us, the members of Duncan's Theater Troupe, sat together in a circle in the first-floor gymnasium. It was our first meeting and our first rehearsal. By the end of today, Mr. Perske would tell us what play we would be performing this semester, and who would be playing which part. Our Troupe auditions had been considered role auditions too—they were how the play's casting would be decided.

As we continued with our breathing exercises, I took a look around the room at who else now belonged to Duncan's Theater Troupe. I saw Dustin directly across from me in the circle, closely following Ms. Miller's instructions. His gaze was intensely focused and he wore a denim button down shirt with blue jeans—a look that could have been too much denim on someone else. On him it just enhanced his natural glamour. The train of thought soon made me distracted and I tried to focus exclusively on Ms. Miller's instructions.

Some of the other kids who were in the Troupe were carryovers from last year—juniors and seniors who now held seniority in the Troupe. They hoped to get the best roles in whatever play we were assigned, having paid their dues last year. The rest were younger like me—sophomores who had seen last year's production of *Guys and Dolls* and vowed to be a part of the next one. I hoped though, that this year there would be no singing. Singing was not my strong suit; I had been thrown out of Marion's Karaoke Studio on two separate occasions.

"Now," Mr. Perske continued, "copy my facial expressions. We want to practice the physical experience of the full range of human emotions."

He contorted his face into extreme frowns, grins, shrieks, and everything in between.

"This is the actor's warm-up," he explained. At first I felt extremely self-conscious, but with the continuous repetition, I began to feel more free and relaxed.

Apart from Dustin and me, there were about ten juniors who had continued over from last year, plus Ramona Kano and Diane Smith, two nice girls I had known since freshman year; the twins Niko and Riley Yardley; and Sawyer Bailey and Charlie Falk, two buddies of mine and Ming's who also liked Art class a ton.

"Excellent work, Troupe," Mr. Perske said. "Everybody take a seat now."

We all sat cross-legged on the gymnasium floor. I eyed Dustin discretely. His raised eyebrows suggested an interest in the announcement that was to come. I couldn't help noticing how his blonde hair fell over his face, and the confidence that exuded from his entire self. I vowed not to be distracted by anything that Dustin or his presence suggested to me.

"So," Mr. Perske went on, "this semester, we wanted to reexamine a very familiar and classic bit of drama. We were very impressed by the talent we saw in this year's auditions and are eager to utilize the talent of those Troupe members who have already been with us."

"We will be performing two plays this year, one each semester," Ms. Miller elaborated. "This semester's play will be debuted right before the Christmas holidays in December, and it will be Shakespeare's classic *Romeo and Juliet*. Who's up for a romantic play?"

There was a mixed assortment of groans and

cheers that erupted from the group. I wasn't sure how I felt about it myself. I mean, what could we bring to that story? Anything new? I wasn't sure about the romantic end of things there. I liked playing tough guy roles.

"We've thought long and hard about casting, based on your auditions, or what we saw in your work last year if you were with us then. So without further ado, here it is. Juliet: Marie Kahn. Romeo: Blake Teller. Mercutio: Dustin Dern—"

Mr. Perske finished reading the casting, but I could hardly hear him. I couldn't believe that I had been given the starring role of this semester's production. Neither could Dustin.

Once my name had been announced as lead and his as second-lead—Mercutio is Romeo's best friend in the play—his face had turned red. A few Troupe members glanced his way to see what his reaction was. Apparently a lot of people had thought Dustin would get the lead part—the part that I had just gotten.

"During next week's rehearsal, we'll work in pairs and trios on individual scenes within the play. If you have not already done so, please read the entire play for next week," Ms. Miller instructed.

Mr. Perske handed out Xerox copies of the scenes we would work on next week. Mine was a scene between Romeo and Mercutio. I would be working with Dustin.

Looking up from the Xerox, I caught his eye and tried to smile at him. Dustin seemed to half-scowl and then turn away. He had really wanted my part. My stomach flipped over once, then again.

This really was a romantic play.

I sat cross-legged on my bed surrounded by my posters of James Dean, Marlon Brando, Matt Damon, and Johnny Depp. These were my favorite actors of all time. One day I hoped to be hanging on some kid's wall—some kid in a tiny attic bedroom in rural Maine, reciting his favorite monologues to the silence around him. Some kid like me.

My Android phone, the oldest model ever because Vera had bought it used, lay in front of me, digging into the soft fabric of my down comforter. I hoped the phone would be absorbed into the bed and disappear for all eternity. Well, at least for tonight. I was waiting for a call that I didn't want to be waiting for from someone I really, really did not want to speak to.

My dad.

It was currently seven twenty-five on Wednesday night. Dad was supposed to call me at seven thirty. I was supposed to answer at seven thirty, Vera's orders.

She had been over the moon when I told her about the play's casting. Thankfully we had no sugary items on hand to celebrate with at the time. That milkshake and cake the other night had sentenced my sweet tooth to death for the time being.

"Call your dad, Blake," Vera had urged me. "It'll make him . . . well, *happy*."

"Why do you care about whether Dad's happy or not? I mean, after . . . what happened?"

Vera shot me a disappointed look, sighing deeply. She didn't answer and walked out of the room.

Our relationship had been vaguely strained since.

I refused to call Dad. He had never even bothered to learn how to text. If something was too difficult for him, Dad just didn't do it. So I followed suit. It would be too difficult for me to call him and tell him about my Duncan High acting career, so I didn't. Like father, like son.

Except my refusal couldn't hold. When your best friend is your mom and you live with your best friend who is your mom, the not-talking-to-each-other bit gets old . . . fast. Two days later, I waited until she was done with her meditation session, then went in and apologized. I told Vera that I would set up a call with Dad on Wednesday night, which was now.

Dad had been overly friendly in response to my cold email, the one in which I asked him when he might be free to talk. He had been this way ever since he split up with Vera. I guessed it was the quintessential guilty-divorced-dad routine. I had seen it in movies before. In the past, Dad had been chill, cool, relaxed when talking with me. He was likeable and I was too and we got along. When he didn't agree with what I said, he told me so. Now I felt like he agreed with me no matter what. He wasn't being real. I hoped to get the call over with in less than ten minutes.

Suddenly my whole bed buzzed; the phone was ringing. It was Dad's 212 number—he was calling from the landline in his East Village apartment that he shared with Audrey.

"Hello?" I said tentatively into the phone.

"Hey, Blake? Hey, it's Dad. How are ya?"

There it was—that immensely blameworthy tone again trying to disguise itself. Trying to pretend everything was okay.

"Hi, Dad."

"Glad to get a hold of you finally! You're one busy guy!"

"Uh, yeah. Sure." I didn't want to get sucked into feeling sorry for Dad. He cleared his throat a few times, in the way that people do when they're feeling extremely self-conscious. I could try and help him out to speed this whole charade up.

"How's your teaching coming? Working on any new pieces?"

I had always liked Dad's sculptures—large reinterpretations of human figures in grey clay. Sometimes he used real flowers, sticking them into the figures' hands. They would dry there until they died, but they still looked fascinating.

"It's wonderful Blake, thank you. I just finished a new piece of a Scottie dog on a leash, except the leash stands in midair because there's no human holder. The dog is modeled after Fitzy, remember him?"

Fitzy was our next-door neighbor's dog when I was a kid, a crazy and aging Scotty dog who didn't like anyone except me and Dad. He had died two years ago.

"Yeah, I do. I miss Fitzy."

Silence. *Make it short and sweet*, I remembered.

Dad wanted to know about the Theater Troupe, so I would tell him.

"I made it into Duncan's Theater Troupe. My audition went really well, and I was cast as Romeo in this semester's play. We have our first real rehearsal tomorrow."

"Wow, Blake, I'm so proud of you. Mom was saying that it's a big deal for a younger student to be cast in a lead role."

"Yeah, it is. Thanks."

"We'd love to come up and see you when the play happens, Audrey and I. She's proud of you too, Blake. I told her all about it. She says hi."

How could Dad be so dumb? Exactly what I did not want to hear. I wished I could wipe all knowledge of Audrey from my mind. The mention of her name just reminded me of Vera locking herself in the bathroom and crying.

"Oh. Well, you should, Dad. I'd like you to." *I'd like to end the phone conversation too,* but who knew when that would happen.

"Listen, Blake," Dad said, his tone growing serious all of a sudden.

"Yeah, Dad?"

"I want you to come down to New York and visit me and Audrey. On a weekend next month, maybe. You can stay with us, we can all go to a Broadway play together on Saturday night, Sunday we can spend the day in Central Park, go to my art opening that night, and Monday you fly home. Well, what do you think?"

I was torn. All of these activities sounded incredible. I had never been to New York, and a Broadway play sounded perfect. But I had only met Audrey a couple of times before. I wasn't overly impressed. Did I really want to spend an entire weekend with Dad and Audrey kissing up to me, trying to pretend like we were all old friends and everything was fine?

"That sounds—potentially nice. Thank you."

"Well, good. Great. We can't wait to have you! I'll take care of the plane ticket and everything—"

"Okay. Thank you," I replied, not sure of how to act. For a split-second I missed us, our original family, how we used to be. Vera, Dad, and I, all joking together, all in the same family together. They used to make me feel just like I was one of them, an artist in arms. Now, I didn't know what I was.

"You don't have to thank me," Dad said. I could tell by his tone that he was embarrassed. "I'd love to see you. We would. I miss you, Blake."

I felt like I was getting choked up. I fought it, though. I wouldn't give in to his guilt trip.

"Miss you too, Dad. I've got to go now. I'll see you in a few weeks."

During the separation settlement, Vera and Dad had agreed on custody rights for me to live with Vera, granting visiting rights to Dad. It was a rational decision and Vera and Dad had agreed easily to it. Dad and I got to decide when and where we saw each other, letting both of us off the hook in terms of any regularly scheduled get-togethers. Dad had tried hard to see me plenty though.

He cleared his throat again.

"Sure thing, Blake. Looking forward to it. Good luck with the play."

I hung up the phone and threw it back into the comforter. I lay down on my bed for a while and tried not to think of anything at all. After that I had to do my Geometry homework.

———

"O Romeo, Romeo!"

"Ha *ha* Ming, very funny."

"Wherefore art thou, Romeo?"

"You're laughing now, but that joke will get real old, real fast."

Ming and I were sitting across from each other in the cafeteria with our friends Sawyer and Ramona, who were both in the Drama Troupe with me. Sawyer and Ramona had been dating since

middle school it seemed like. They were this estab-
lished inseparable couple that everyone at Duncan
was extremely used to. I had always liked Sawyer.
He did these incredible charcoal drawings of night-
marish figures, half-based on people he knew,
half-based on film characters. He had been given
the part of Benvolio in the play, Romeo's cousin
and wise friend. Ramona played a general chorus
member in most of the scenes.

"It's such a big deal that you got the part of
Romeo, Blake, really," Ramona said as she played
with Sawyer's hair.

"Yeah, everybody's talking about it. It's the first
time a sophomore's gotten the lead, like, ever. You
must have had some audition," Sawyer said.

I thought back to the audition moment; it had
been one of my best readings ever.

"Well, I did try awfully hard," I agreed,
grinning.

"Dustin must have, too. Mercutio's a great character," Ramona said.

Ming raised her eyebrows at this. I felt my face grow kind of hot. Suddenly I felt extremely nervous. I cracked my knuckles.

"Kendra said he's absolutely devastated over not getting Romeo," she went on.

"Devastated? Really?" Ming asked in disbelief.

"He's disappointed, anyway," Sawyer added. "He really wanted the lead."

Suddenly I had a flash of trying to work with Dustin in scenes—scenes in which he wanted my part. What if he sabotaged everything I tried to do? Actors were supposed to trust other actors; they were supposed to feel safe working with them, safe to be honest and vulnerable and all that. Would I be safe around Dustin?

"Mercutio's a good part," I said, wishing the subject would change.

"You know," Sawyer added, munching on the crust of his PB&J, "there is that romantic vibe in the text, between Romeo and Mercutio. I wonder if Ms. Miller will bring that up."

"What romantic vibe?" I asked, suddenly feeling nervous. "They're just best friends."

I hadn't signed on for that kind of thing.

"Well, traditionally," Sawyer went on, adjusting his eyeglasses and sitting forward in his cafeteria chair, "the friendship between Romeo and Mercutio is up for analysis."

"Like any friendship between any two people," Ming interjected, slightly annoyed.

"Anyway," Ramona added as the bell rang, "don't get sucked into Dustin's world."

We all got up and gathered our knapsacks, textbooks, and trash. What could Dustin's world possibly be like?

"Dustin's world?" I asked. "Don't worry, it couldn't happen."

———

"During this Troupe rehearsal," Mr. Perske told us, "we'll spend time on individual scene work. Some of the most pertinent scenes in the play, when rehearsed in depth, will allow us to grow closer to our characters. So you all have your scene assignments for the afternoon, correct?"

Ms. Miller had handed them out moments ago. Today, I would be working on a major Act One scene with Dustin.

"Now, you can use one of the empty classrooms on this floor. But you should feel comfortable with your scene partner, with space and enough privacy in which to do some powerful scene work. Okay, everybody? It's now three fifteen. Let's reconvene back here at four thirty to compare notes," Ms. Miller instructed.

The Duncan Troupe players dispersed. I looked across the room to Dustin, who was reading his scene papers carefully.

"Hey," I said, aiming for cooler-than-cool in my approach. "Wanna try Ms. Miller's office at the end of the hall? Bet everybody forgot about that one."

Dustin looked up at me; he seemed nervous. "Okay."

We walked slowly together away from the gym and down the long corridor. As we approached the end where the office was, all sound and activity from the Troupe died away behind us. It was quiet now and I felt safe and secure.

Dustin strode through the room and sat cross-legged on Ms. Miller's desk. I smiled at his brazenness but remembered to keep my guard up, too. I didn't want to get sucked into Dustin's world just yet.

"So," he said, eyebrows raised, "want to start with just reading it through?"

It sounded like a good idea. I had re-read the entire play in the past week, and even worked with Vera and Ming on memorizing some lines. But reading through with a fellow actor would be another experience.

"Sure," I agreed, taking a seat in the chair opposite Ms. Miller's desk. "Works for me."

We began to read through the scene, and I was immediately struck by how good of an actor Dustin was. As he spoke his lines, it seemed as though he was Mercutio. It didn't seem like he was acting. Mr. Perske had said in the Troupe's introductory meeting that as actors, we should feel that standing up on stage and reciting our characters' lines should be enough. In other words, that was acting—speaking the lines as ourselves. Any extra add-ons were unnecessary; confidence was all a person needed. Dustin had it. No wonder he'd wanted to be Romeo. Suddenly I wondered why I had gotten it instead of Dustin. Did Mr. Perske and Ms. Miller really think I was a better actor than he was? Was I?

When we had read the scene through I could tell that Dustin was impressed with my delivery as well. We looked at each other across the office in silence, unsure as to what to do next exactly.

"That was really great," Dustin said jumping down from Ms. Miller's desk and stretching his legs. "Have you worked on memorizing the scene at all?"

I stood, too, ready. I had memorized the scene; I had worked on it all week.

"I have, yeah. I think we should try it off-book. The sooner, the better."

Dustin nodded seriously and I tried to follow his mood. I was intrigued by the raging increase of my heartbeat while spending time with Dustin. It was entirely new for me.

I threw my pages to the right and they landed on a nearby desk. Dustin did the same thing. We started the scene again.

This time there was nowhere to hide, nowhere else to look. The white Xerox pages of our script could not help us. Dustin and I had to be real to each other, whatever that might mean.

We stormed all over the room; we pushed each other; we laughed at each other; we stared into each other's eyes. It was easy because we weren't Blake and Dustin; we were Romeo and Mercutio. We were other people. We were free.

The scene that Mr. Perske and Ms. Miller had assigned to us was the well-known scene around Mercutio's speech: "I see Queen Mab hath been with you." In the scene, Mercutio tells Romeo that he must have been dreaming, and Mercutio talks about what dreaming is. It was one of my favorite scenes in the whole play.

When Dustin delivered his last lines in the scene, he reached out and grabbed my hand. We stayed like that for a few moments. In the play we were supposed to be best friends, and for a moment I kind of wished we were in real life. He seemed like someone I could relate to.

"Want to run through it again?" Dustin asked, pacing around the practice room and running his hands through his hair. He seemed intense and focused on the task at hand.

"Sure, why not?" I agreed. The clock on the wall

read four fifteen; we had just enough time to run through the scene again.

"Maybe this time we could switch parts?" he added nonchalantly.

"Switch parts? Well, what for?"

I felt nervous. Would Dustin try to steal my role? Could he do that even?

"Yeah, one of my old acting teachers used to have us do that as an exercise. Plus, I've got tons of ideas for Romeo's lines in this scene."

Tons of ideas? I didn't have tons of ideas on how to play Mercutio; I had trusted Dustin to do that.

He eyed me from across the room and suddenly his confidence really annoyed me.

"Why don't we come into the scene from two different points, outside of the room?" I proposed. "I don't want to switch parts."

Dustin was pacing back and forth, cracking his knuckles in anxiety.

"What are you doing?" I asked Dustin.

"What?" he looked into my eyes, distracted from

his focus. "Oh, I'm getting revved up for the scene, that's all. We don't have to switch parts; it's fine."

I sat down in a desk chair for a moment, feeling exhausted. I usually felt like this when I worked on my monologues, but it seemed amped up when working with another person.

The rehearsal room that we were in had two separate entrance doors, one at the front and one at the back. There were no windows.

"How will I know when to come in?" I asked, vaguely nervous.

"You'll hear me speak first," Dustin assured me. "I'll come in first. It's just so we have a chance to clear ourselves out, get back to neutral, so that we can approach the scene with a maximum amount of energy."

He sounded very official, almost clinical. But the scene work was going well, even though Dustin was increasingly getting on my nerves.

I walked to the far side of the room and left through the door to wait. I paced back and forth, willing myself to get more into character. I wanted to impress Dustin and I wanted to impress myself.

I heard him slam his door open and come bursting in with his first lines of the scenes; I followed and did the same.

I had never seen Dustin with such charisma. We went through the entire scene as if we spoke the lines ourselves, off the tops of our heads, interrupting each other, cutting each other off. We reached the end of it and were standing so close to one another, I could feel his breath on my neck.

The scene had ended but we kept looking into each other's eyes. I felt kind of sick, like I might pass out. I wanted to run from the room but my sneakers were glued to the floor. I didn't know whether I hated him at the moment or—

"Well, that was great!" Dustin exclaimed. We still stood close; Dustin hadn't moved an inch.

4

Neither of us budged. We were still extremely close to each other and I wasn't sure what would happen next. The feeling was exciting, exhilarating, and terrifying.

This was all well and good; it was artistically satisfying, in fact. But the intense feelings that I felt at the moment seemed to reach far beyond the scene we were rehearsing. Suddenly we weren't Romeo and Mercutio any more. We were Blake and Dustin.

His gaze burned through mine and I couldn't look away. Someone needed to say something; *I* needed to say something. My mouth was dry and I was frozen on the spot. I tried just the same.

"Well, that was, not bad. Really . . . on point," I tried.

Dustin just looked at me. I felt at home under his gaze, as though he wasn't judging me or trying to figure me out or anything. He was just letting me be—for a while anyway; who knew when his arrogance would come bursting through and ruin it. Who knew how badly he had wanted that lead role and how jealous he was of me for getting it.

"Time's up, guys," a voice from far off said suddenly. Dustin and I were brought back to the present reality, the one with four walls. Mr. Perske stood in the doorway with his notes clipboard in hand.

"Okay? We're reconvening in the gym before rehearsal comes to a close. How'd it go?"

Dustin and I looked at each other and then started putting our scripts into our book bags in silence.

"It went really well, I think," Dustin answered. He shot a sidelong glance my way.

"It did, Mr. Perske," I added.

"Great! We—Ms. Miller and I—felt you two would have great chemistry as the best friends of the play, Romeo and Mercutio. It seems we were right."

Was this chemistry? I wondered. Suddenly the fluorescent lights seemed extra bright, like I couldn't hide anywhere. I still wasn't sure what had happened between Dustin and me. Did he like me or not? Was he just acting? Was I just acting?

That said, there was most definitely something else, another intense emotion hanging around me like a cloud that wouldn't disappear on its own. I wasn't sure I knew what it meant. I had only felt it once before—last year, when I was dating this girl, Anna, who was in Eastport for the summer. She was a year older than me, and she wanted to be an actor, too. We met in Mom's store; I was working there a few days a week and Anna came in looking for one of the new terrible beach reads that was popular that season. We got to talking and the next thing I knew, we were spending tons of time together, and then we were dating.

We would go to the movies at night and then to the diner for shakes. When we kissed, whenever we were together, I felt on edge, as though I didn't know what would happen next. The summer had ended and she went back home to Trenton, and that was the end of that. But Dustin had brought this all back to mind.

The fact that Dustin was a guy and not a girl made me feel . . . uncomfortable. I worried more though, about what people would think about us. What if we liked each other? Would Dustin and I date? Would we be romantic together? Would we kiss? What would everyone at Duncan High School say? What would Ming say? What would Dad and Audrey say? What would Vera say?

This was assuming Dustin was heading in this direction with me. Maybe he was just trying to charm me so that he could blindside me and steal the lead. Ramona had said that he was seductive. Maybe I was reading into our moments in too intense a way. It could be my loneliness talking.

Since Dad moved to New York and Vera became more withdrawn, I had definitely felt more on my own. It wasn't just Dad and Mom that had gotten divorced, it was our entire family. It had always been the three of us, and with them splitting up, I was also set apart from our former trio. Working with Dustin now on the Troupe material, it was impossible not to fall for the opportunity to get close to someone, to get close to Dustin.

As we rejoined the Troupe in the gym, the vibrations were at a positive high throughout the room. It seemed that the rehearsals had gone well. Marie, who would be Juliet, was laughing hysterically with Diane, who would be playing Nurse, Juliet's confidante. I was excited to rehearse the rest of the scenes in the play, and I was excited for our families and friends to watch the finished version, although we had a ways to go before then.

"So, we hope all of your scene workings went well," Ms. Miller said to us from the front of the room. "This way of rehearsal is wonderful for the preliminary stages such as these, and we hope it will allow you to connect to your characters and to those with and around you."

I felt my cheeks turn red as I stole a glance at Dustin. He had only had one boyfriend before, whom I knew of, anyway. It was some guy named Tad, whom he was always raving about to Kendra. Dustin called Tad his ex, so they were no longer together, as far as I knew. Tad hadn't gone to Duncan. He was the son of Dustin's dad's law partner. Maybe whatever was going on with Dustin and I wasn't a big deal to him. But it was to me.

I felt myself getting attached. I worried that I was getting tricked.

I had just been given the lead role in the semester's play. If I started to fall for Dustin, how could I give my full attention to the play and to getting into character? How could I convince the audience that I was in love with Juliet?

"We're going to continue rehearsal like this for the next few weeks, working on individual scenes, before we begin to string the whole play of acts and scenes together. Good work today, everyone," Ms. Miller said.

I grabbed my book bag and ran out toward the main hangout zone, near the entrance of Duncan. Ming was there waiting for me. She was the vice president of the Duncan Painters' League, and her meeting had been that afternoon, too.

We usually walked home together. This particular afternoon, I had a lot that I wanted to discuss.

"Ming?" I started, as we slowly walked toward Main Street, the point from which we could head to our respective homes easily. Ming and I lived a few blocks away from each other, but a lot of afternoons I walked her home first. Her house was on the way to mine, so I didn't think much about where we were walking.

"Ming, what do you think about Dustin?"

We walked along the deserted main roads of Eastport. Ming was quiet and then cleared her throat a few times. She always did that when she was nervous or overthinking something.

"He's fine, I guess," she said. "He's obviously adorable, looks-wise. But I don't know him that well, really. Why are you asking? You've been rehearsing with Dustin. Wouldn't you know more than me?"

I stayed quiet, pondering. Sure, of course. Ming was right. But I still wanted to hear her thoughts.

"Sure," I said, "but in general, what do you think about him? Is he cool?"

Ming raised her eyebrows in a defeated sort of way.

"Well," she said, "of course he's cool. He's a stand-up guy, in an individual way. He's nice. And I'm sure he's a good actor."

We walked along for several moments.

"Is that what you wanted to hear?" Ming clarified, clearing her throat.

"Well, yes, sure," I said. "I'm just not sure about him myself. Not sure how I feel about him."

"What do you mean?" Ming asked. "As your character? I'm sure Ms. Miller would be happy to—"

"No, not Ms. Miller. For some reason it's been tough to be neutral toward him. I know in the play, Romeo and Mercutio are these best friends, so it's probably good if we have some sort of relationship."

We walked along past rows of homes—white and blue houses with windows shuttered against the damp evening breezes. I sniffed the air; I sensed a storm coming. It made me feel edgy and uneasy. Ming furrowed her brow in thought.

"Well, sure. You've got to get used to that, I think, right? If you're gonna be a big-time actor, Blake?"

She was treading lightly on something that felt very heavy and confusing to me. We came to the small playground at the end of the block; it was empty. I led us toward it and we sat down at one of the picnic tables. I suddenly missed Dustin. I wished I had his number to text him. I wondered what he was doing now.

"Sure, Ming. I guess what I'm trying to say . . . " I hesitated. I hesitated to say something I had never spoken out loud before. Maybe Ming would think I was a freak and never speak to me again. Maybe I *was* a freak.

"I think I'm attracted to Dustin. I like him as more than a friend. I think I might like guys. I mean, I don't know for sure but lately—well it's occurred to me."

My heart beat relentlessly fast in my chest. There, I had said it, and the world had not come crashing down around me. I was still alive. But what would Ming think?

"Okay, well, that's . . . interesting. Dustin is really good-looking and charming. I'm attracted to him. Have you liked other guys before, too? That's totally cool . . . but, well, what about Anna? You dated her, you liked her a lot, remember? Maybe it's just Dustin you like, not . . . all guys."

Ming scanned my face for answers in her calm and caring way. She sounded just as confused as I felt. I could tell she was a bit surprised but trying to be relaxed about it. I had never told her anything like this before.

"I did like Anna a lot, but it never felt like this. This feels so . . . intense. It feels out of my control. It scares me. I don't know what's going on, Ming."

I felt tears of frustration gather in the corners of my eyes. I had liked Anna in a light way. We got along and had fun together. Holding hands with her, kissing her, was easy, fun, something to do. It didn't compare to Dustin. Between us was this intense, impossible-to-ignore energy whirl. I kept remembering how he held me that night outside Mom's store. I wanted him to do it again. That moment had felt real. But now that we were involved in the play, who knew how real either of us was being?

"That's okay, Blake. Don't worry about it. I mean, you don't have to understand exactly what's going on. Just let yourself . . . chill, for a while. See how the rehearsals go. See what happens."

We reached Ming's house and she opened the front gate to go in.

"Remember how nutso I got over Andrew last semester?"

I smiled to remember it. Andrew was Duncan's resident rebel, a wild kid who had been Ming's lab partner in Biology class. She was obsessed with him for months. Eventually she told him how she felt and he told her that he didn't want to be tied down. Ming was devastated and didn't eat for a week. Then she got over it. I couldn't imagine getting over Dustin.

"Sure, Ming."

Maybe she had always suspected something like this would happen with me. Or perhaps she was right—whatever I was feeling about Dustin wasn't worth being scared of. It was easier said than done.

We hugged goodbye and I watched Ming walk through her front door. I wished I could feel as relaxed about the Dustin thing as Ming seemed to be.

I picked up a stick from the ground and drummed it along the white picket fences as I walked toward my house. I had a Geometry problem set to finish when I got home, which I was not looking forward to. Since joining the Troupe, I hadn't been focusing too much on my class assignments. The less I thought about them, the less I wanted to do them. The less I wanted to do them, the less I actually did do them. But I was determined to not fall behind in my work. Ms. Miller and Mr. Perske had a policy on grade point average: to remain in the Troupe, a member had to consistently maintain good academic standing. It was a good motivator I supposed, but it was not the most fun rule to follow through on.

I wanted to work on memorizing some more of my lines for the play once I got home, too. In the next rehearsal we would be spending half the time finishing up the scene work we had already done, and then spend the other half moving onto another scene with another partner. Then I would start working with Marie, my Juliet.

Maybe it's just Dustin you like, not . . . all guys, Ming had said. I didn't really know. I had never thought about it before, not until Dustin. But now that I did start to think about it, a lot of things made sense if I considered the possibility of being attracted to guys.

When I was with Anna, something about our time together never felt right. I thought it was because I wasn't over the moon about her, which I was aware of at the time. We were friends and spent a lot of time together. I could tell she liked me a whole lot, more than I liked her, which was fine. Then, one night when we walked home from the movies, she held my hand. When I walked her home to her house, she kissed me. Then we considered ourselves to be dating.

But we were really young. I know it was just the previous year, but still. I didn't know myself as well then. I had liked kissing Anna, but it always felt kind of just okay. If she hadn't made a move on me, I don't think I would have made a move on her. I was just there.

I wanted to make a move on Dustin. But did this mean that I liked guys now? Did a person have to decide that kind of thing in an official and outright way? I had never thought about declaring that I liked girls.

I reached my front door and saw Vera's bedroom light on. I walked around to the back of our house and sat in the rear porch chair. I didn't feel like going in just yet. My conversation with Ming, while somewhat relieving, had not satisfied my need for discussion. I wished I could talk to Vera about it. I didn't know how I could. I had no idea what she would possibly say. She had been a model; she had been married to a sculptor; she had lived in New York City. I assumed she was open-minded about most things, but I didn't know if that would carry over to where I was concerned. Especially since I didn't really know what was going on either.

I just felt strange, and I couldn't stop thinking about Dustin. I was almost scared to see him again. How long could we go on ignoring the elephant in the rehearsal room?

5

I rode my bike the long way to school the following Thursday morning. I had left early, before Vera had even woken up and made me breakfast. The night had been a long and uneasy one, and I hadn't slept well at all.

I had only seen Dustin twice since our last rehearsal—once on Monday, in the far hall by Principal Royce's office where he was stuffing his Chemistry textbook into his locker between classes. He didn't see me as I stood near the next bank of lockers over, watching him. Dustin wore black jeans and Converse, and a light pink Oxford button-down. The light in his eyes, in his face, was always the same as it was in that moment—open, bright, warm. Seeing him at a distance like that made me realize how attached to him I felt. It was probably just from working on the play with him so much. Yes, it was probably that.

Dustin slammed his locker door closed, grabbed his book bag up off the floor, and headed toward the stairwell. But then Schwartzman was there suddenly and blocked his way. There weren't too many idiots in Duncan High, but he was one of them.

Schwartzman was a jock—the meanest guy on the soccer team, not sharp enough to be captain. He pushed Dustin from the back and caught him off guard. Dustin tripped and his textbook went flying. I was about to go over and tell Schwartzman he could take a flying leap, when I heard what he said to Dustin.

"Watch where you're walking, Dusty. Hey, I heard only weirdos wear pink. That true?"

Schwartzman walked off laughing as the late

bell rang. It was the hurt in Dustin's open eyes that really got to me. He didn't look angry with Schwartzman, just disappointed. Quickly he stood up, brushed himself off, and went on his way. It occurred to me that this was not the first time that something like this had happened to Dustin. It then occurred to me that if I continued to allow my feelings for Dustin to get out of hand, as they seemed to be doing lately, this kind of thing could happen to me. Schwartzman could trip me up in the hall one day, call me "weirdo," and walk away laughing. The thought terrified me.

The second time that I saw Dustin was outside Loretta's Market on Water Street. It had been around dinnertime the previous night, Wednesday night, when Vera had asked me to go buy some olive oil for the salad that she was making. I was coming out of the shop when I spied Dustin and Kendra going into Omar's Coffee next door. He almost didn't see me but then he did, and instead of saying hello or waving, he looked away and hurried into Omar's.

It was funny; since working with Dustin on the play and attempting to figure out what I was feeling about him and what it meant for how I viewed my own identity, I hadn't considered what he might be going through. I could tell that he was also feeling at least some version of the vibes between us, and that probably left him feeling weird, too. I could imagine Dustin having a crush on me because I knew he was gay, but maybe it was a stretch for him to imagine I might have one on him. It was more of a mental risk. But then, weren't most crushes?

I rode my bike up to my favorite high hill that overlooked the sea below. The familiar feeling of wanting to escape came flooding over me. Looking in every direction from the hill, I could see the entire circumference of Eastport. I looked at my town, realizing how well I knew it, and I wanted to go to a place I didn't know so I could see that. I thought of Dad and Audrey in New York and felt mad at them for the umpteenth time for leaving me behind. I wanted to be where Vera was, but I also wanted to feel free. Looking at my watch I saw that it was eight o'five, which meant that I had only ten minutes to get to Homeroom. I sighed, knowing that given the hypothetical distance between any two points in town, there was no way that I could be late.

The day at Duncan seemed to race by, and each class I went to threw more and more homework assignments in my lap. Normally this wouldn't have bothered me a ton, but the further I went into drama study, the less time I had to do anything else.

The thing was, I didn't really want the day to race by. It was Thursday, and the Troupe had rehearsal after school. Dustin and I had to rehearse our Mercutio-Romeo scene again. And I wasn't sure what was going to happen this time.

During our last rehearsal, whatever was going on between us had hit some kind of max. The emotions in the room scared me. They might just have been the results of a scene well done, dramatically speaking, but I suspected that wasn't it.

That afternoon as I turned the hall corner, on my way to the usual classroom that Dustin and I rehearsed in, Mr. Perske stopped me. He was slightly out of breath as usual and held his reliable clipboard close to his chest.

"Blake! I just wanted to remind you that we will only be spending half the rehearsal time today on your current scenes. Then we'll move on to others, and you'll finally get to work with Marie. You'll finally get to be with Juliet!"

Mr. Perske beamed. The thought of spending less time with Dustin was relieving but also terrifying. Artistically speaking, it would be great to work with Marie and try to build some ease between us. I had only spoken to her a bit here and there. She was a junior at Duncan so we had never had any classes together, other than the Troupe.

Mr. Perske looked a little disappointed with my lack of a reaction. I tried to muster an appearance of enthusiasm, hoping to convince him. I seemed to, because he patted me on the back in encouragement.

"Exactly, Mr. Teller, exactly. Best of luck on your scene work."

I turned the knob on the classroom door and walked in, slamming it behind me. I leaned against it and took deep breaths, feeling like I had just escaped from something. I saw Dustin sitting at the grand piano—it was the music room that we practiced in—hammering out "Mary Had a Little Lamb" with an index finger. I was a few minutes late.

"Hey, Dust," I said, aiming for nonchalance and tossing my backpack to the side of the piano bench. "How've you been?"

He looked at me, still playing the piano, with tired eyes.

"So-so," he answered, as he stood up and walked toward me. When Dustin got closer, I saw that one of his cheekbones was slightly bruised, accompanied by a minor scratch.

"Hey," I started, "what happened to you?"

"Schwartzman," he answered neutrally. "He got to me in the hallway on my way over here from Chem. Tripped me up and I slammed my face into the corner of my locker door."

I felt irate, my fists clenching slowly. If Schwartzman had been in the room with us, I would've pummeled him. Had he really bothered Dustin again?

"That idiot," I exclaimed. "Did you tell . . . Mr. Perske? The principal? Schwartzman can't get away with that!"

Dustin stood up and brushed his clothes off with his fingertips.

"Trust me," he said, "it's not worth the trouble. It'll just happen again. Don't worry though, I'll get him back."

I was silent for a moment, thinking. Was this

what Eastport was like? No wonder Dad had escaped to New York.

Dustin cleared his throat and skimmed through his scene notes.

"Ready?" he asked me. "Now we only have a bit of time for this last run-through. Then you're off with Juliet and I'm off . . . I don't know, really. Rehearsing with Tybalt, probably. I do love a good swordfight."

There was something so admirable about the way in which Dustin dealt with Schwartzman's bullying. He reacted more in a general disappointment that went beyond Schwartzman as an individual. Like a disappointment in the human race, yet it didn't turn him into a bitter kid.

We put our scripts to the side and ran through the scene. It was incredible, the best version of it that had ever been. The best of our rehearsals, the best of all the rehearsals that had ever been since Shakespeare wrote the thing. Now I felt sure that Dustin wasn't trying to sabotage my performance even though he had wanted the part. How could the scene be so good if that were true?

I had heard about actors having moments like this one. I had read about it, too. Every once in a while a scene would fall exactly into place and take on a subtle sort of magic. It would feel to the actors and seem to the audience that the lines being spoken were being spoken naturally, off-the-cuff, for the first time in human history.

This success was most likely the result of our numerous run-throughs, going over the same scene again and again during rehearsals so that we were almost numb to it, allowing us to re-inject it with our own truth. Yes, that was it, I was sure, and yet . . . and yet . . .

"Wow," I exclaimed, still frozen in my closing pose of the scene, inches away from Dustin. "That was really great."

"Yeah, I think it was, Blake," Dustin replied, breaking character and pacing casually about the room. He wore a red flannel shirt and dark jeans and his curly blonde hair had gotten longer so that it stuck out every which way. He looked irresistible to me, the realization of which made me feel semi-woozy.

It was funny, liking Dustin this much, in this way. It felt fine there in the rehearsal room; it felt light and good and real and true. It was only when I started to factor in Vera, my Dad, Ms. Miller and Mr. Perske, Ming, and Schwartzman that I wanted to hightail it out of this place on the very next Greyhound. Maybe that was the issue with anything that ever involved trouble— wondering what other people would think about what you most wanted to do. What a dumb way to live your life. But it was easier said than practiced.

"Boys?" a voice said from the doorway to the classroom. It was Ms. Miller. "Time to move on to your next rehearsals. Mercutio, Tybalt's waiting for you across the hall. Romeo, Juliet should be here in just a moment."

Dustin picked up his bag and headed slowly

toward the door. When he reached it, he turned to glance back at me.

"I'll see ya later, Blake."

I felt like I might crash through the tiled floor below me, but just then, Marie came in. Dustin said hi and then disappeared into the hallway behind the door. Ms. Miller followed him.

"Hey, Blake," Marie grinned at me. She was tall and angelic-looking with white-blonde hair and big eyes, and something about her was very relaxed, putting me at ease instantly. I liked her, but she wasn't Dustin.

"Hey, Marie," I replied.

"Do you want to start on our first scene together, when we first meet at the party?" she asked. "I haven't quite memorized it yet."

I was relieved; neither had I. The play was five acts long, after all, with a lot to memorize, and we had time before December's performance.

"No worries," I told Marie, "neither have I. Let's try running through it, anyway."

The scene was the fifth and final scene in Act One and would set the tone for the whole rest of the story; it had to be convincing. We had to amp up the over-the-top flirting; we had to seem like we were really falling in love.

Marie was a good actress; that much was obvious as soon as the scene began. Her delivery was natural, almost understated, and she read her lines like they were modern twenty-first-century lines. I was impressed.

This was the scene where Romeo first kissed Juliet, and when we got to that point in the scene, I froze. I hadn't kissed a girl since Anna and that had been a while ago. I wanted to be a professional actor, the best. I wanted to be a James Dean—smooth, confident in the character. But I froze.

Marie waited a second or two and then broke character; I could tell she was nervous too.

"Why don't we just . . . skip that bit for now?" she suggested.

"Good idea," I replied, trying not to sound too relieved.

We ran through the scene two more times, skipping the kiss each time.

As good as Marie and I were, and as well as we worked together so far, I couldn't help longing for Dustin again. There was something about his and my energies that blew everything else to the wayside. Marie and I had more restraint between us. With Dustin, it seemed like my emotions could go further and further and keep on going, like there wasn't any way to keep them in check. This scared me . . . a lot. Mercutio and Romeo's relationship wouldn't get the amount of stage time that Juliet and Romeo's would.

At five o'clock Mr. Perske came in and told us rehearsals were done for the day and that he would see us next week.

"I think it's going to be really great, Blake," Marie said as she grabbed her text from the piano and walked toward the door. "You're a good actor."

She turned red when she said this. Suddenly I got the feeling that Marie had a crush on me.

"Me, too," I hastily agreed, trying to seem neutral but friendly. "You're a great actress. The play should be the best Eastport's ever seen, if we keep this up."

Marie smiled and left. I grabbed my bag and walked down the hall to the exit doors, exhausted. All of the emotions I had seemed to have risen to the surface during this rehearsal and twisted a bunch of different ways. Maybe I would take up meditation like Vera suggested.

As I unchained my bike from the outside rack, I felt a tap on my shoulder. Dustin. My heart beat so loudly I swore that he could hear it.

"Hey, are you doing anything Saturday night? I have an extra ticket to the show at the Arts Center on Main Street. Wanna join?"

Dustin was nervous, almost like he was asking me against his better judgment, but waited intensely for my answer. The afternoon breeze whipped his hair this way and that.

How could I say no to this guy?

I would meet Dustin at Bernadette's Pizzeria at six o'clock on Saturday, and then we would go to the play at seven thirty. This had all been decided over text on Friday afternoon.

It was now six ten and I stood outside the place, pacing back and forth in the prematurely cold winds.

Dustin was late, or he wasn't coming at all. I chose to believe that he was late.

I had to believe this because I had convinced Vera that going out with Dustin was more important than going to dinner at her friend Sam's house, where she was spending her Saturday evening. She had wanted me to go with her, and I would have if I wasn't seeing Dustin. I liked Sam a ton. He had the hots for Vera, but I approved. Sam was the coolest guy over forty in Eastport.

When Vera heard that it was a play we were going to see, and that it wasn't just any play but one of her favorites, Tennessee Williams' *Suddenly Last Summer*, she encouraged me to go.

"It's one of the best plays in modern drama, Blake. You have to see it performed live," she told me, tossing our dinner salad in her favorite wooden bowl on Friday night.

"I know that, Vera. Which is why I want to go. Not that the Eastport Players are a guaranteed display of artistry or anything."

Vera shot me a disapproving look.

"Blake, remember what we figured out a while back?"

We had decided that any practice of a person's creative talent was a good step in the right direction. An actor shouldn't perform to get fame, money, or accolades, but instead to practice his craft alone. To become a better artist. And it didn't matter where or when a person did this. In other words, the Eastport Players and the Royal Shakespeare Company were on the same level . . . in theory.

"Who are you going with again?" she asked me as we sat down at the kitchen table. I hadn't really told her about Dustin, not in any real detail. I felt self-conscious when I thought about Dustin, let alone talked to other people about him. So far my conversation with Ming had been the most I had verbalized.

"The kid from my theater troupe," I answered. I tried to observe whether she looked suspicious, since I usually would tell her more than this.

"Oh, yes, that's right, Austin." She wasn't suspicious at all.

"Dustin," I corrected, stuffing a forkful of salad into my mouth.

"Right," Mom said. "Are you getting a bite to eat first, or should I set aside something for you before I go out?"

"Bernadette's," I answered, mouth still full.

"Blake, I told you not to do that, you could choke to death for goodness' sake."

———

So now I was pacing back and forth in front of Bernadette's waiting for Dustin to show. I felt nervous and excited, kind of like when I used to wait for Anna to show up on our dates. But this feeling tonight was worse, much worse. My teeth kept chattering and it wasn't all that cold. I had to calm myself down before Dustin arrived.

Even for a Saturday night, Bernadette's wasn't seeing too much action. In the fifteen minutes I had waited, only two groups of people had gone in for dinner. Eastport's Saturday night was probably like a Monday night in New York. No, not even that busy.

Why was I so nervous about meeting Dustin anyway? He was just a person, just a fellow actor, just a kid I knew from school. Like meeting Ming for dinner . . . except I never got nervous about that.

I shook my hands out in front of me to try and let go of the crazed-up feeling I had. Vera hadn't been suspicious at all about my going out with Dustin tonight. Why should she be? I felt strangely guilty about the whole thing, like I should be keeping something about it secret. I did have a tendency to be overdramatic at times, of course. But the whole thing just felt so true to me.

Just like that, there he stood in front of me, out of breath and smiling. Dustin looked incredible in a motorcycle jacket, t-shirt, jeans, boots, and light pink scarf. He stomped up the three steps of Bernadette's porch to where I was standing.

"Hey. Sorry I'm late, I . . . long story. I'll tell

you about it when we sit down," he said, hugging me hello.

I hadn't hugged him since that night outside Vera's store, the night that I felt my whole world was falling apart. Tonight I felt like that again, but for entirely different reasons.

"Let's grab a table," I said, holding the door open for us.

I had always loved Bernadette's, and their pizza was maybe the best thing about Eastport. We took one of the wooden booths by the window. Dustin ran his fingers through his hair, recomposing himself.

"Did you walk here?" I asked, not having seen his bike.

"Yeah, I live about two blocks over, on Glenn."

Glenn Street was a bit run-down, with half its houses nearly falling apart.

"But I was late because," Dustin went on, opening his menu, "the babysitter for my little sisters was late showing up. She babysits them all the time, but she never remembers our address. I don't know why my mom hires her, she's so ditzy. And she always gets lost on her way over. Eastport doesn't have that many streets! How can somebody get lost in it?"

I swore I could listen to him read grocery lists. I only hoped I had the same kind of charisma.

"How old are your sisters?" I asked. I didn't really know that much about Dustin.

"Eight and ten. Are you cool with pineapple pizza?" he asked over the menu.

It was the only way to eat it, as far as I was concerned. I always had to make my case for it with Vera or Ming. It was nice not to have to for once.

"It's my favorite," I answered him.

"Wow, magic words. I always have to explain why pineapple pizza is the best. It's nice not to have to do that," Dustin said.

We stared at each other and smiled for a moment too long, and I suddenly got self-conscious. I needed to change the subject.

"Do you see a lot of the plays at the Arts Center?"

"No, not really," Dustin said. "I saw Sam Shepard's *True West* last year, one of my favorite plays. The production wasn't very good though. What I really want is to see something on Broadway, again. You know, New York."

"Me too," I agreed quickly. "My Dad moved there last year."

"Really, your Dad lives there?" Dustin's face lit up, like I had just told him the best news ever.

"What'll ya have?" a voice spoke. It was the waitress, there to take our order.

"Small pie, with pineapple," Dustin said. "And ginger ale, I think."

"Me too," I added. Vera didn't allow soda into the house, so I always ordered it in restaurants.

Dustin focused his attention back on me.

"So, your dad's in New York; you must be there all the time, like every other weekend!"

"Well," I tried to explain, "not really, no. I

actually haven't been there to visit him since he moved. He's living there with some woman now."

"Really? I would be there like, every weekend! He's got a place there, right? You could stay with him? Man oh man!"

Dustin was incredulous and very impressed.

"Yeah, well, it's not quite like that for us. We don't talk that much since he moved out. I can't stand spending time with his girlfriend, Audrey. It's not worth it to me. Though I have to visit them soon."

Dustin listened attentively. "What's the girlfriend like—Audrey? Why can't you stand her?"

It was strange being asked the questions I had continually asked myself in my own mind since Vera and Dad split. It made me reconsider the whole thing, kind of. I grew angry, thinking of the words I was about to speak.

"I can't stand her because she's the reason why my Dad left. He would still be with Vera I bet, still living with us here in Eastport. Couldn't she find some other guy to date? Why'd she pick my married dad? Now she's got him. And me? I'm trying to keep Vera, my mom, happy when I can."

Just then the waitress came over with our pizza, slamming the silver platter down onto the tiled tabletop. Dustin and I gave each other a look.

"Maybe you could try and keep the wait staff here happy too. Seems like they need it," he said, before cracking up. I started to laugh, too. I had been so nervous before meeting him there that now I just felt exhausted. I laughed to relax, not because what Dustin had just said was so funny. I hoped I wouldn't fall asleep during the play.

Dustin reached forward and served me and then himself a large slice of pizza.

"I get it," he said, about to take a bite of his slice. "I was mad at my dad too, when he first divorced my mom. I don't think he had a girlfriend at the time, though. I think he just wanted out."

I was dumbstruck. I had known Dustin lived

with his mom and sisters, but I had never thought about how his dad had left.

"Your parents are divorced? Do you still see your dad?"

Dustin smiled up at me, raising his eyebrow charmingly.

"Yeah, since I was little. I see him twice a year. He moved to Alaska a long time ago."

He seemed to be full of surprises, and more like me than I realized.

"But," he went on, "my dad was the first one who got me interested in acting. And when I told him I was gay—"

I looked up sharply; this was the first time he had mentioned this to me specifically.

"—he was really great about it. Surprisingly. I mean beforehand, I imagined horror story versions of that moment."

I wasn't sure how interested or disinterested I was supposed to seem at this moment. Was I supposed to ask questions? Was I supposed to act like it wasn't a big deal? It wasn't, to me.

"To be honest," Dustin went on, "living in Eastport isn't the worst. Most people are accepting; some of them are even cool. There's only one Schwartzman, which is good."

We each reached for the last slices of pizza.

"I mean, what do you think about it?" Dustin asked me. I wasn't sure how to answer. Luckily, the waitress came by with the check then. Dustin reached for it to review it, then into his pocket to take his wallet out.

"This is probably the most expensive place in Eastport," Dustin said as he threw a twenty down. I did the same.

"I know," I agreed. "Hey . . . did you really want the part of Romeo when you tried out for the Troupe?"

"It wasn't Romeo I wanted, it was the lead, whatever the lead was. But I didn't get it. Happens sometimes. I was really mad about it at first but I'm over it now."

As soon as Dustin had spoken he looked over at me, like he'd caught himself being too honest. I was glad I had asked, because I couldn't quite shake the fear that Dustin getting closer to me was a trick or something.

"My ego was out of whack, you know? Actors' egos are *the worst*. But I have to admit you are a great Romeo. Better than I would've been."

Dustin looked at his watch and raised his eyebrows.

"Wow, it's seven ten already. We should get going."

How could I have worried about Dustin trying to *steal my part*? I felt so dumb suddenly. Still, there was no doubt that Dustin's initial anger and my fear had made our rehearsals more emotional, more tense.

Now I was starting to feel like the only time I

was myself was when I was onstage pretending to be *other people*—and when I was with Dustin.

"How'd you get the tickets?" I asked Dustin as we left Bernadette's and took a right toward the Arts Center. I left my bike there, planning on going back to retrieve it after the play.

"Easy," Dustin said. "I bought them at the box office. I don't think the Arts Center has sold out any show its entire existence."

We approached the theater's main entrance, amidst several other ticketholders.

"How much do I owe you, then?" I asked him as we were led to our seats in the balcony.

"Don't worry about it," Dustin said, furrowing his brow as we were shown our seats by the usher. "It cost like ten dollars. I wanted you to come with me; I'm glad that you did."

Sitting next to me, Dustin smiled and grabbed my hand, giving it a good squeeze before letting it go. I felt my face flush a deep shade of red. I was sure I had never liked anyone this much in my entire life.

The play passed by quickly. At intermission, I bought Dustin and myself a bag of red licorice from the concession stand. We devoured it on even terms. When the last act was over, and the cast members took their final bows, Dustin insisted on walking me to my bike, which was still at Bernadette's Pizzeria. As we walked the two blocks, Dustin brushed his hand against mine, then held it. I tried to think of something to say, to confirm the nonchalance of the moment.

"It was a pretty good show, right? For the Eastport Players?"

"True," Dustin agreed. "It's nice to know that if we never make it out of Eastport alive, we have a chance of getting an acting career going here, too."

We reached my bike and I bent down to unchain it from its post. I looked up at Dustin.

"Well, thanks so much, Dustin. For everything. I had a great time."

He looked into my eyes and then quickly pulled my face toward his, and kissed me.

I had never kissed a guy before, and it was almost exactly like kissing a girl, like kissing Anna. But better. I felt closer to Dustin than I had felt to her.

He pulled away and looked at me again. I felt so exhilarated I could hardly focus.

"I really like you, Blake."

I thought about it for a split second, then pulled him toward me.

"I like you too, Dustin," I replied, kissing him back. Suddenly I heard rustling behind me and I pushed him away in fright.

I turned to see the grove of trees outside the theater, rustling their leaves in the wind. It wasn't anything at all, but I wondered why I was so bothered by my surroundings. I just wasn't sure I wanted anyone I knew to see me making out with Dustin yet. What if Schwartzman showed up and saw us? I'd have to resign from Eastport and move someplace else.

"Can I see you again? I mean, can we hang out again? On our own time like this, not just in rehearsals?" he asked.

Dustin stood inches away from me, his arms around my waist, awaiting my response.

"Yep. I'm in."

"How was the play?" Vera asked me from her spot on the sofa in our living room. She was watching an old Cary Grant movie on television, just having gotten back from her night with Sam.

I threw myself down next to her.

"Fine. Yeah, great. The actors were pretty good, considering they were just the Eastport Players."

I wanted to tell Vera about the other part of the night; I wanted to tell her about Dustin.

"Sam made an incredible salmon dinner, with

Swiss chard and the works. He played this great jazz music on his new stereo system too. He asked for you, sends his best."

She yawned, clueless of what I wanted to tell her about Dustin and me.

"How was Dustin?" asked Vera. "Did he like the play too?"

Now seemed to be the best time to tell her what had gone down. Vera, even though she was my mom, was my closest friend. I hated keeping things from her.

"He did," I answered, fidgeting in my spot on the sofa. Here went nothing.

"It was great to see him," I went on. "We've really been connecting during rehearsals lately, you know, in an artistic way. And it was cool just hanging out with him for kicks. It was cool that we were able just to be ourselves, to get to know each other more."

I looked at Vera with her tired eyes glued to the Cary Grant film. He would know how to handle this moment with class and charm and ease. I tried to channel him as I ventured forward.

"I think we really like each other, you know? I think we really . . . click."

Vera picked up on my tone and muted the television, turning her gaze to me.

"Well, that's wonderful, Blake. You should have him over soon."

I felt frustrated. I wanted to get it over with.

"Yeah, I will, Vera, but, I don't think you get it. I think we like each other, Dustin and me. Like in a . . . romantic sort of way, you know? I think I might . . . I think I might like guys."

I said those last six words kind of fast and I wasn't sure if Vera had heard . . . until she looked at me in a frozen stare. She'd heard.

She seemed to be in shock and I wasn't sure what to do. I was so nervous I wasn't sure I could stand up.

"Vera?" I asked. She got up abruptly, went into her bedroom, and shut the door behind her.

Since my Saturday night conversation with Vera—if you could even call that a conversation, me revealing very important personal news to my mother, only to have her leave the scene without so much as an acknowledgment of what I had just told her—I couldn't stand to be in the house.

I had gone up to my room and cried into my pillow after that. I felt totally confused about the entire night and Vera freaking out on me just made everything worse. We were always there for each other; whatever happened, whatever we felt, it was always okay to tell the other. We had a safe space between us that way. But what I had told her about Dustin, and that I could be gay, wasn't accepted. I had no idea what Vera was thinking because she hadn't told me, so I was forced to assume that the idea was repulsive to her.

As I was crying into my pillow, I heard a text come in on my phone and looked to see who it was from. Dustin.

Had a great time tonight ;) See ya at rehearsal!

It just made me more upset. I had had a great time too, but now I wasn't so sure I wanted to see him at rehearsal. How could this situation get any better? How could Vera ever come around to being okay with me dating a guy?

I didn't answer the text, and I spent my entire Sunday doing homework at the Eastport Library. When I got home around seven that night, Vera had left a plate of dinner out for me with a note that read "Gone to Sam's, I have my cell." That was all. What was she thinking? How did she imagine I felt? Wasn't she worried about me at all?

I left early for school on Monday morning, much earlier than I usually did. I wanted to take another bike ride around Eastport to clear my head before going to class. The wild air was freezing, and I zipped my windbreaker as high as it would go.

Pedaling my bike around our house and down by Water Street, I hardly saw another soul. Once again taunting me, I saw the morning Greyhound bus pull out of the station and down toward the main road.

One good thing about spending yesterday at the library with my classwork was that I felt very prepared for school. For a Monday, this was impressive. By devoting long and uninterrupted hours to work, I had gotten into—yes, almost excited about—the material I spent time with. This material included advanced algebra problems, a bunch of grammatical exercises for my English class, Chemistry equations, and outlines for two longer-than-long chapters in my Global Studies textbook. I was exhausted by the time I got home, which I used as an excuse to go to bed early, before Vera even got home from Sam's.

I was exhausted by more than just the intense study session I had put myself through.

I had wondered about the possibility of liking guys. In the past, whenever I thought about it for more than a couple of seconds, I became anxious and scared and forced the idea from my mind. I had never had much interest in or luck with girls, but I had never wondered if there was a reason. Especially once I met and became involved with Anna, I really forced the idea out of my mind. I had liked Anna a lot and felt very close to her emotionally, and the physical interactions we did have were always pleasant and nice. I still wasn't sure whether I could classify myself as gay or not, either. The only romantic experience I had with a guy was with Dustin.

On Sunday morning I had googled about how a person would know this kind of thing for sure, which turned out to be not the best idea, because the internet is full of just as many psychopaths as it is with smart, well-meaning people. There were theories to support every possibility, which was how my own brain felt and it didn't help. A bunch of theories offered no certainty.

I didn't know what I was; I didn't know how I would define myself; I didn't know whether I could. Maybe I just liked individuals, and it didn't matter what gender they were. But then, why did I like Dustin to such ridiculous levels? Why did spending time with him, thinking about him, acting with him, make me so nervous? What was that, if not the biggest crush I had ever had on anyone in my entire life?

Dustin was so charming and handsome. He was seductive and sexy too. And I would have said that about him no matter what gender he and I were. I mean, it was more or less fact. Why did I have to make a decision or definition about myself now, when I hadn't had to before? People never "come out" as being straight. Why was being gay a big deal—if I *were* gay, that is?

I had probably rushed into the "coming out" thing to Vera too soon, but I needed to tell someone about how the night had gone and she was the first person I ran into. I would have told her about me and a girl, if the same night had happened with a girl instead of Dustin. I doubt that she would have reacted the same way; in fact, I was certain she wouldn't have.

I felt terrible that I hadn't answered Dustin's text. If I were him, I would be very confused. What if he never wanted to speak to me again? What if we had to work on the whole rest of the play without talking to each other?

What if Vera never wanted to speak to me again either? What if we had to spend the whole rest of our lives without talking to each other? How would that be? I didn't see how it could be; I'd have to move in with Dad and Audrey. New York would be great, but living with them—I really did not want to do that. And this was assuming that Dad would be okay with the idea of me and Dustin romantically involved. This was getting to be like a game of dominoes; I had never thought so much about how my actions could directly affect everything and everyone else in my life. I felt insecure, frozen, stuck.

I rode my bike down by the water for a while, circling and circling the same pathway. Then I made my way over to Duncan. As I locked my bike on the rack outside, I saw Dustin heading toward the front entrance with Kendra. She was talking so loudly that I could catch echoes of her harsh tone on the breeze, even though there were dozens of other students around. Dustin seemed to be only half-listening to her as he gazed absentmindedly in my direction, then focused on me. He didn't look away this time but instead smiled confidently and waved hello to me. Everything he did made me like him more. He could've acted weirdly with me, now that I had ghosted his text, but he didn't.

I waved back at him and was about to go over to say hi, when Ming came up from behind me carrying about ten textbooks.

"Here . . . take . . . some . . . Blake . . . please—"

I took half the stack off of her hands as she breathed a sigh of relief. They weighed a ton.

"Jeez, Ming, what are these for? A new weight-lifting program? How were you carrying ten?"

"Sheer willpower," she answered, motioning with her head to follow through the main doors.

I looked for Dustin but he must have gone inside with Kendra.

"Actually," Ming said over her shoulder, "I'm bringing them in to Mr. Walker's classroom for him. I volunteered, which may have been a mistake."

We took the books into the empty classroom, the one Mr. Walker never used before second period. I slammed my stack down on his desk and Ming did the same.

"I'm surprised he let you take all of them,"

I said, trying to catch my breath. "What was he thinking?"

"He said I would need help, but I was trying to show off."

Ming walked to the window and looked out at the yard.

"Wow, the grass is even drier-looking than last year. Why do we live here again?"

I walked over to join her at the window.

"Because we're kept here by our parents, by force."

"Not forever, though," said Ming, looking hopefully up at the sky outside. "Hey, how was your weekend? How was the play? How was Dustin?"

She raised an eyebrow at the last bit. We hadn't really spoken any further about Dustin or my recent realizations, but I guessed we would now.

"Fine," I answered. "Great. The Eastport Players are actually kind of . . . good."

"*They were?*" asked Ming doubtfully. "Huh.

So . . . what'd you guys do? Just see the play and go home?"

"Yeah. Well, we had pizza first too."

"With pineapple?"

"Of course," I said smiling.

We were quiet for a minute. I hoped Ming would drop it. I didn't feel like talking about Dustin because I wasn't sure what was going on.

"Did anything, like, happen? Was it . . . a date?"

Yes, something happened. Yes, it was most definitely a date. I shrugged my shoulders.

"Nah, not really. Don't know."

Ming scowled. She knew me better than this.

"Blake, come on. You're really not gonna tell me anything? We always talk about our dates to each other!"

I looked into Ming's eyes and suddenly realized now dumb I was being. Whatever had happened between me and Dustin, whatever was happening, wasn't a big deal. Right?

"Fine, Ming. Yes, it was a date. Yes, we made

out. And that's all I'm giving you, because that's all that happened—"

Ming jumped up and clapped her hands fast like an excited kid. She reminded me of Kendra.

"Oh my God, Blake, oh my God! What was it like? Is Dustin fun on a date, I bet, right? Is he charming and all that? Is he romantic?"

I rolled my eyes at her but laughed. I'd forgotten that Ming had a crush on Dustin too.

"Jeez, Ming. Next time you can come along with us, how about that?"

"Are you guys officially, like, dating now?"

I suddenly remembered leaving Dustin's text unanswered and wished I hadn't. The first period bell rang, and Ming stood up, rubbing her back in pain.

"Those textbooks might have been a bad idea," she said, heading for the door.

"You think? I don't know if we're dating now. I don't know what's going on. It's still all very new, and thus, could go either way."

Ming cracked up as she headed down the hall.

"A few weeks of Shakespeare and you're dropping *thuses* in regular conversation? Nice. I'll see ya later."

When I got home after school, Vera wasn't doing her meditation but instead sat at our kitchen table, waiting for me. A plate of her chocolate chip cookies was set out in front of my seat. She looked more regular, more neutral, than angry. Still, my instinct was to bypass the kitchen entirely and go straight to my room.

"Blake, sit down a minute. I made your favorite cookies."

She sounded a bit formal. I knew what our conversation would be about, if we had any. I took my seat and tried to act as naturally as possible.

"How have rehearsals been coming along?" Vera asked me.

I took a cookie and stuffed it in my mouth.

"Fine. Yeah, great. I'm rehearsing the Juliet scenes now, with Marie? She's pretty good."

"I can't wait to see the play!" Vera answered, a bit too quickly. "And, how's your other friend . . . Dustin?"

I nearly choked on my last bit of cookie.

"Oh, I don't know, haven't really seen him since. He's fine I think."

Vera sighed and sat back in her chair.

"You know, I talked with Sam . . . about what happened with you on Saturday night—"

This annoyed me. Who the hell was Sam to say anything about me or my life?

"Oh yeah? And what did the Wizard Sam have to say about it?"

"He said that this kind of thing is very common with teenagers, and that it doesn't necessarily mean that a person is, you know, gay."

I didn't know what to say and she went on.

"Did you guys have beer or something? Because sometimes—" she asked.

"No, Mom! No we didn't. Don't talk to Sam about me so much, okay?"

Vera stood up and went to get a glass of water from our Brita pitcher.

"I know with your father and me living apart, it hasn't been easy for you. Maybe you're acting out like this—"

I stood up abruptly.

"May I be excused, Vera?"

"Blake, this isn't one of your scenes. You can take it down a notch."

I was so angry I wanted to kick my chair over and get right on the afternoon Greyhound.

"I'm not acting out, Vera, and I don't think I'm in a play right now. I'm fully aware that this is reality. You don't know how it was on Saturday night. You weren't there, you don't know Dustin. You don't know what I'm going through. You have no idea."

Vera's eyes looked sad. "Blake—"

"I'm never telling you anything again, ever!"

I ran to my room and slammed the door. Vera

didn't come to see if I was okay, like she usually did when we had a fight.

———

"Maybe we should do it with the kiss this time? I mean, if we're gonna do it that way in the performances, we should get used to it in rehearsals . . . right?"

Marie stood before me in our rehearsal room. It was Thursday again. We had just rehearsed the *Romeo and Juliet* party scene, the same one that we had rehearsed the previous week.

"You're right," I agreed, setting my script to the side. I tried to ignore how nervous Marie seemed. "Let's try it."

We did and when we got to the kiss, I just went for it—slightly nervous myself, but trying to believe for the moment that I really was Romeo and that kissing Juliet was the most natural thing in the world.

But it didn't feel that way. It felt like acting. All I could think of was Dustin. I couldn't help it. And then all I could think of was Vera and what she had said to me. Then I just felt sick.

For the second half of rehearsal that day, Ms. Miller and Mr. Perske had us all come together to show each other what we had been working on. We only had time to go over two or three, and I hoped my scene with Dustin wouldn't be one of them.

So of course it was.

I had seen Dustin show up for rehearsal and quickly looked the other way when we made eye contact. I was so freaked out by Vera's opinions that I wasn't sure how to be around Dustin. Paralysis or running away had become my standard reactions.

When our names were called, Dustin and I walked to the front of the gym to perform our Romeo-Mercutio scene. I felt hyper-aware of what anybody might think of how we acted together, even though we were supposed to be acting as other people. So instead of the intense chemistry that had been undeniable in our rehearsals, and on our Saturday night date, this run-through had none. I had never performed so badly in my life. My line delivery was borderline monotone, and I looked Dustin in the eye maybe once during the entire scene. It would have been hard to believe Romeo and Mercutio were neighbors, let alone best friends.

When we were finished, there was a moment or two of silence, then hesitant applause from the rest of the Troupe. I saw Niko mouth "Yikes!" to Riley as she slowly clapped her hands.

"A little shaky, a little shaky, but getting there surely!" Mr. Perske assured us. I felt embarrassed and wanted to get out of there, fast. I wanted to be alone.

When the other scenes were finished and Ms. Miller dismissed us, I ran outside to unchain my bike, and was just about to take off when Dustin came running over.

He was literally the last person I wanted to see at the moment.

"**B**lake, hold on a minute, will ya? What happened back there?"

Dustin was all out of breath and wore a confused look on his face.

"I mean," he went on, with his hands on his hips and looking around, "you froze up. It was . . . weird. Is it because of Saturday?"

I looked into his eyes and felt like crying. Why was this so difficult?

"I don't really want to talk about it, Dustin."

He rested his hand on mine, which leaned on

my bike bell and made it ring. He pulled it away nervously and laughed.

"Why not? Didn't you have fun on Saturday? I thought you did. I thought we did."

I tried to answer him but I felt all choked up.

"I did, it's . . . it's Vera, my mom. I told her about us, and she's been acting weird. She thinks I don't know what I'm doing. She doesn't think it's real. Now she's talking to her boyfriend about me. I feel like I have to keep running away."

Dustin grabbed my hand, his manner serious.

"You don't have to run away. It's confusing for me too; I've never felt this way about anybody before. And . . . if this is the first time you've hung out with someone like me, a guy, like this, it's gonna feel, like, different to you, you know?"

I hugged him tightly. Suddenly I heard a voice shout out.

"Hey looks like the Queen of Duncan High found his other queen! That you, Teller?"

It was Schwartzman, riding his bike away from

the entrance. He was laughing hysterically, the idiot. I wanted to shout back to him to shove it, but Dustin ignored him.

"How about your dad, Blake? Have you tried talking to him about it, about us?"

"I haven't tried talking to him about anything since he left, really."

Dustin flashed that irresistible smile at me.

"Maybe you should."

———

Dad picked up on the fourth ring, and I cringed in response. I had been hoping he wouldn't pick up and I could leave a voicemail instead. Then I could tell Dustin I had tried to talk to Dad but it just hadn't worked. No such luck. I paced back and forth in my room, looking to my James Dean poster for moral support.

"Hello, Blake? Is that you?"

Dad's voice was worried, concerned.

"Yeah, it's me. Hey, Dad. If you're busy or something right now—"

"I'm not busy, Blake. Is everything okay? Are you alright?"

I threw myself down on my bed and tried to relax. Was everything okay?

"Sure, Dad, I'm fine, I guess. Can't I just call you to say hi?"

He sighed on the other end of the line, sounding tired.

"Of course, you know that. I'm just surprised. You hardly ever call me. I call you, and I usually call the house because you never answer your cell—and even then, I can almost hear Vera dragging you to the phone."

I always thought I was so clever about that, too. Suddenly I felt badly about how I had treated Dad since he left. Then I remembered Audrey and the feeling went away.

"Well, I've been busy, with the play and everything," I said, clearing my throat.

"Sure, I know." Even over the phone I could still hear the guilt in his voice.

"It's been going well; rehearsals have been going well."

"That's great to hear, Blake. I can't wait to see the play. Audrey and I were just talking about it again this morning. She's excited for you, too."

Come on, Dad! Why did he always try to bring her into everything? Didn't he understand I didn't care about her one bit? I didn't say anything, so Dad kept talking.

"Good news on the Scottie Dog piece, the sculpture of Fitzy. Remember I told you last time we spoke?"

I wasn't sure how I was gonna tell him about Dustin without it being some kind of big news—which I did not want it to be, because I didn't even know what the news was exactly.

"I remember, sure."

"Rumpelmeyer wants it for a group exhibit he's

doing at Smyth Gallery next month. It should still be on when you come to visit us."

Oh, right. I had forgotten about that.

"Congrats, Dad. Sure I'll see it. So, in the Troupe at school, we've been working scene by scene. So far I've worked with this girl Marie who plays Juliet; she's really great. And this other kid, uh, Dustin? He plays Mercutio, a great actor."

Maybe the worst conversation segue of all time. Dad seemed a bit caught off guard but tried to follow my thoughts.

"Wow, that's a nice way to do it, I think. You probably get to know each other well that way, too."

You really do, I thought.

"Yeah, well, I've been hanging out a lot with Dustin. We get along, you know?"

Boy, I hoped this wouldn't end up like it did when I told Vera. At least Dad couldn't leave the room like Vera did; he'd have to hang up on me, which seemed worse somehow.

"Well, that's nice, Blake. You'd want to give Ming some time off anyway. You two were as thick as thieves when I left Eastport."

"Still are," I said forcing a laugh. "Yeah, Dustin and I saw a play over the weekend at the Arts Center. Went to Bernadette's for pizza, too."

Come on, I thought to myself, *just say it. Get it over with.*

"He's the one who told me to call you tonight, actually."

"Really? Why?" Dad asked, surprised.

"He said it would help me . . . sort things out. See, Vera and I, we haven't been on great terms lately."

"Oh no Blake, what happened? I can't imagine that—"

"She's upset that I went out with Dustin."

Not the whole truth maybe, but I was getting there.

"Well, why would Vera be upset about that? Is this kid, Dustin—"

"He's gay, Dad. And something happened when we were together. We . . . we made out. And now I think I could be gay too, I'm not sure. I told Vera and she flipped out on me . . . Well, she walked out on me anyway. And Schwartzman at school saw us together today . . . and I have no idea what I am or what's going on here. Dad, I'm scared."

I let out a huge sigh of relief. No matter how Dad reacted now, I had told him. There it was.

A few seconds passed by, then I heard Dad sigh, too.

"Well don't be scared, Blake. Don't do that to yourself. At least you're being honest."

"So you're not mad at me, Dad?"

"Of course not, Blake. I wish . . . I wish I was there with you, in Eastport. We could spend some real time together and talk."

I thought about it. Maybe it wouldn't be such a bad idea after all. Maybe he could talk to Vera about things, too.

"I'd be up for that, Dad; I could use it right now, to be honest."

There was silence on the other end of the phone. I could hear him thinking.

"Audrey and I were supposed to go antiquing this weekend in Connecticut. Maybe we'll come to Eastport instead?"

I frowned to myself.

"You're going antiquing now, Dad? Since when?"

"Audrey's been very into it recently—"

"—and I don't think I really need to see Audrey any time soon."

Dad sighed again. "Blake, I think it would be good for us all. You don't have to talk to Audrey if you don't want to."

"Okay. Sounds good."

I looked up at my James Dean poster again. He would've been proud of me for calling Dad, for agreeing to let him see me this weekend, for not running away from situations when they got tough, like Dad had done when he moved out, or like Vera was doing to me now. Dustin would be proud too.

———

"Blake, what are you doing?"

Ming and I had just sat down in our Global Studies seats for Mr. Walker's class, our last of the day. We had made it all the way through the week—one more class and we were home free. It was Friday.

I was now staring at the clock on the wall, willing its hands to freeze or at least slow down a bit. I didn't want this class to end because I didn't want the school day to end. When it did, Dad—and Audrey—would be waiting outside to pick me up. They were on their way to Eastport right now.

"I'm trying to use my mind powers to freeze time, okay, Ming? It can't be that difficult."

Ming groaned at me and took out her books,

stealing glances at Mr. Walker at the front of the room when she could. The girl had it bad.

"It'll be fine, Blake," she assured me. "It'll at least have to improve things with Vera, right? Somehow? Maybe your dad can explain things to you."

Right, how could Dad really push past his guilt over how he had left Vera and me high and dry for some random woman in New York, and help me with my problem? Didn't he have enough of his own problems? Although . . . well, at the moment, things with Vera couldn't really get any worse.

We were barely speaking, and she was spending many more late nights at the store, or over at Sam's house. The next time I ran into Sam I planned on giving him a piece of my mind, because I was sure he was not helping my side of things. What would fix Vera and me was a real conversation about Dustin and me, during which she would apologize for overreacting and during which I would once again explain that I didn't really know what I was experiencing with Dustin either. That it wasn't a done deal. That we liked each other but were figuring our feelings out as we went along, like any new couple. That I didn't know if I was gay now, if I had always been gay, or what. I just didn't know.

"I hope you're right, Ming."

Strangely, Mr. Walker's class flew by and before I knew it, Duncan's final period bell rang through the halls. My stomach did somersaults as I slowly put my books away and began to walk toward the exit. I had never been so turned off by a Friday afternoon in my whole life. I walked so slowly that by the time I reached the end of the hallway, I felt like the last student left in the building. People usually ran out like the building was on fire.

I stopped at the final door to peer through the glass plate window, which offered a full view of the school parking lot outside. There they were.

Audrey stood leaning against the car trunk and smiling, while Dad paced back and forth in front of her, brow furrowed and waving his hands in the air. He seemed to be as nervous as I was. Maybe this wouldn't be so bad. I stole a glance at my reflection in the plate-glass window, running my fingers through my hair to smooth it out. It was looking less James Dean-ish and wilder lately—out of control, kind of like a mirror of my life. I tried to flatten it down a bit, sighed in frustration, and then made a beeline for Dad's car.

"Blake! It's so great to see you, buddy," Dad said, hugging me tightly. His hair was greyer, his eyes more tired than I remembered. He looked older and it made me feel a bit nervous, like I was missing time with him. I would just keep seeing him for a weekend or two every six months until he was a grandpa one day.

"You too, Dad. Thanks for coming all this way." Still, after I had told him about me and Dustin over the phone, it was hard to look him in the eye.

Audrey came forward and hugged me, too. She had way too many teeth.

"Hi, sweetie. We're so glad to see you."

Even though Dad looked older, Audrey somehow looked younger. The last time I had seen her it had been on a holiday and we were all dressed up. She had worn high heels, makeup, and her blonde hair all done in a princess-y 'do. Today she wore torn jeans, Keds, and her hair was all messy hanging down her back. She looked like she could be one of my friends. Her warm manner reminded me of Vera's—pre-Dustin of course.

"Ready to see a great film, Blake? If we hurry, we can make the four o'clock," Dad said as he got into the car. "Do you want to throw your bike in the trunk?"

"Nah, didn't bring it today," I answered, getting into the back seat. We were headed to the Eastport Movie Theater to see the revival show. Each week a different old movie was screened alongside the new releases, and this week it was one of my man James Dean's films, *East of Eden*.

The ride to the theater from Duncan was only two or three minutes long. Still, it seemed like forever because no one talked for a while. Finally, Dad asked how rehearsal had gone the day before.

"Fine," I answered. "More scenes with Juliet. Now we're into some heavy stuff in the third act."

Actually, we were right up to some of Dustin's main scenes in that act, set for group rehearsal next week—his big death scene and my swordfight scene with Tybalt.

"That's so fantastic that you're playing Romeo, Blake. Your dad and I are so proud of you," Audrey told me over her shoulder, from her seat next to Dad.

Was she trying to trick me, to make me think her and Dad were my parents? If so, it wouldn't work.

After the movie, we went to dinner at Bernadette's. I was starving, so Dad ordered two pizzas for us—one with pineapple and one vegan pie, on Audrey's request.

"You know, Blake," Dad told me between mouthfuls of a slice, "the scene where James Dean offers the money to his dad . . . you know when he comes in distraught, and kind of falls on his dad crying, holding the cash in his hands?"

"The best scene in the movie? Dad, how could I forget?"

He nodded enthusiastically, reaching for another slice.

"Well, Dean improvised that entire part. I mean, it wasn't in the script, really. And Raymond Massey, the actor who played Dean's dad, was totally taken aback by it during filming, because he was old-school. He couldn't stand Dean's style."

Audrey ate her slices with a knife and fork, of course, slowly and deliberately. It was annoying.

"So have you spoken anymore to Vera about your friend, Dustin?"

Here it was, the moment I had been dreading.

"Only for a minute on Monday, when she tried to explain to me some stupid theory her stupid friend has, about how what happened to me and

Dustin was just a phase I must be going through or something."

Dad put his pizza down and looked at me; Audrey did too.

"The truth is, I don't know myself," I continued. "I never thought about being straight or gay that much before Dustin, really. I liked Anna a lot when we were together. And when I started rehearsing with Dustin, I could feel the attraction between us. It was more than just us being buddies, too. It was physical, we both felt it. And then we went out and . . . and made out . . . and I'm not sure. I would be more sure, or I could be, if Vera hadn't flipped out on me the way that she did. Or if Schwartzman, this big idiot at school, wasn't always making fun of Dustin for being gay. It's just . . . I think I can't begin to know how I feel, completely, until I feel like it's safe to feel it—until I know people like Vera or Schwartzman won't bother me about it one way or the other."

Audrey took a deep breath and spoke to me.

"You know, Blake, the same thing happened to my brother Cliff in high school. He tried to come out to our parents and they gave him a hard time. I just remember him worrying about having to tell people, to tell us, that he was gay because he had an experience, a relationship with another guy. I told him then what I'll tell you now. You don't have to make that kind of statement—that decision—now, unless you want to. That kind of moment is for other people, you know? For their benefit. Why don't you take some time getting to know this kid . . . Dustin . . . a bit more. See what happens, see where your friendship, your relationship goes. Just allow it to be."

Dad stared at Audrey, smiling appreciatively. I was too, against my best intentions. It was probably the smartest I had ever heard her sound. Maybe she wasn't so terrible after all.

"We're all just people," she went on, reaching for another slice to cut daintily with her knife and fork.

"And it's natural to like, to desire, to love, other people. You know?"

"I thought you didn't like pineapple," I pointed out. Audrey shrugged.

"Maybe I do and I just don't know it. Hey, it's possible."

We pulled up to the house at around eight o'clock. I held a box with the unfinished Bernadette's pizza. Dad and I both got out of the car, even though I had told Dad that he didn't need to walk me inside. He wanted to speak to Vera though, and there seemed to be nothing I could do to stop him. This would be interesting; I hadn't seen them together in my house since the day before Dad had left for good.

By the looks of it, however, Vera didn't seem to be home. Every light in the house was turned off and I could hear the kitchen wind chimes rattling softly in the evening breeze. I had let us in through the screen door with my key and now we stood in the living room, not sure what to do or where to go.

We had dropped Audrey off at the Eastport Inn on the way back from Bernadette's where she was staying for the weekend with Dad. Dad had told her to come with us but Audrey had said that she had to catch up on her work emails. I think she just didn't want to have to be in the same room as Vera, which I did not blame her for.

I eyed Dad as he shifted from side to side awkwardly, uncomfortable in his own house. Well, I guess it wasn't his house anymore.

"You want to take a seat, Dad? Wait for Vera to get home? I'm guessing she's at Sam's for the billionth time this week, but she usually doesn't stay too late."

"That's okay, Blake, thanks. I'll just . . . stand."

I went to the kitchen to get us some of Vera's sparkling water, watching Dad in the reflection of the microwave glass above the sink. Tears sprung to my eyes, seeing him back there. For a minute I pretended that the past year and a half had been a dream, that he still lived there with us. Why did he have to go and fall for Audrey when Vera and I needed him?

"Bobby, is that you?"

I jumped almost a foot in the air and nearly knocked the two glasses of water I had just poured clean over.

Vera was standing a few feet away from Dad, in the doorway to her bedroom.

"Yeah Vera, it's me. It's nice to see you. We didn't think you were home," he said, keeping his cool. I was still trying to get my breath back.

"Vera, I thought you were out with Sam," I said, walking over toward where Vera and Dad were. These were the most words I had spoken to her in a while.

She looked at me, her eyes vaguely distant and slightly hurt.

"No, I was meditating, and I must have fallen asleep. What time is it?"

Dad looked at his watch. "Eight fifteen."

Vera came into the living room and threw herself on the couch, rubbing her eyes and widening them to wake herself up.

"How was the movie?" she asked us. "Did you eat something, Blake?"

"We took him for pizza at Bernadette's, Audrey and me," Dad answered, sitting across from Vera in my rocking chair.

Vera looked over at me quickly, then looked away once she caught my eye.

"The movie was great, Vera. James Dean was even better in this than he was in *Giant*," I added.

"You still meditate every day then, huh?" asked Dad, folding his arms over his chest and smiling.

"That's right," Vera replied, smiling back at Dad.

They looked at each other for a few moments that way. It was every divorced kid's dream. More than Dustin, more than an Oscar for Best Actor, I wanted Dad and Vera to be together again. I wanted it to be like it was when I was growing up, if only to have someone else to bounce off of when things got tough. I was an only child, and with Dad gone, I had no one to roll my eyes at in response to Vera's antics.

But suddenly I remembered how messed up Vera was after Dad moved out. All the late nights she had spent at the bookstore. Hearing Vera shout, "You're living with her?" at the top of her lungs into the phone the day Dad didn't come home. The way Vera couldn't really explain what had happened right away, how I was forced to piece it together myself. The way I heard Vera whisper to Sam one night at dinner a few months ago when I came along, that she *never would've divorced* Dad if he hadn't insisted.

It was all Dad's fault. Which was why I was mad at him in the *first* place, why I had been mad at him since he left, why I never wanted to talk to him on the phone or visit him and Audrey in New York. He had torn our family apart and we could not be fixed now. And then the guilt in his voice, the easy way he tried to carry on light conversation with me about his sculptures, the easy way he tried to carry on light conversation with Vera here, now. Like nothing had ever happened.

Well, it had happened. It happened to Vera and me.

"You can't just do this, Dad," I said loudly. He and Vera were caught off guard and turned to look at me. "You can't pretend like everything is okay here."

"Blake what are you talking about?" Vera asked. She seemed to be more awake now.

"Well," I began, my anger rising, "Dad here hasn't been home in months; he hasn't been part of this family for months. But he acts like he is tonight. You, Vera, haven't been speaking to me normally for the past week. I have recently announced, to both of you, that I have an intense crush on my scene partner Dustin, who is in fact *a guy*. We may be getting romantically involved. I don't know what that means. I don't know if I have to come out now or something. Yet you're both pretending that it's not really an issue when of course it is. When are we going to talk together, really talk? I mean, when are we going to say it like it really is?"

I was crying now but managed to keep my cool amidst the tears. It felt like all of the rage, frustration, confusion, and longing that I had pushed down underneath me for months were now rising to the surface.

"Blake . . . Blake, I'm so sorry," Dad said, quietly—so quietly that I had to lean forward to hear him. He had a faraway look in his eyes, like he was just now seeing the havoc he had wreaked. It occurred to me here that all of this would be great emotional material to draw on for my scene work.

"I know it hasn't been easy for you this past year—for any of us, but especially you," he went on. "It wasn't your decision, yet your whole life was affected by the divorce. I'm sorry about that Blake, I truly am. We both are," Dad went on.

Vera shifted her gaze from me to Dad and back again, her hands over her mouth in shock. I was kind of in shock myself. I hadn't let myself think these thoughts, let alone speak them or hear them spoken by Dad.

"It's okay, Dad," I replied, full on crying now. I went over to him quickly and hugged him, getting tears all over his jacket. "It's just, *I miss you*, that's all."

Dad sniffled slightly too but tried to make it seem like he wasn't. He pulled away from me and put his hands on my shoulders, the way he always did when he was about to give me instructions.

"Well, I miss you too, Blake! I wish you'd call me once in a while—or at least answer when I call. And you should come and visit Audrey and me in New York, every weekend if you want! We could see a different Broadway play every week!"

Vera cleared her throat and tapped one foot in annoyance.

"Every weekend, Bobby? I'd like him here at least some of the time."

"Sure, of course. I'm just pointing out to Blake that there are ways of staying close to each other, and being involved in each other's lives, even though I don't live here anymore. Now, what about this Dustin character?"

I groaned unintentionally, not wanting to discuss Dustin at the moment. I had managed to forget him while Dad rambled on.

Vera had been watching me but when I caught her eye she looked away. I threw myself down on the sofa.

"Vera thinks it's just a phase I'm going through—or *Sam* thinks so anyway. But it's getting hard to tell the difference between the two."

"Blake, don't say that. I know my own mind. Only you know what you're going through, I was just trying to point out to you the other night that . . . you shouldn't be in such a rush to make a big decision like that. One experience with one person doesn't necessarily redefine your identity. It doesn't necessarily mean you're gay. I just wanted you to feel like you had options."

This annoyed me. First of all, Dustin hadn't felt like a decision to me one bit, just like Anna hadn't felt like a decision to me. The hook-ups, the relationships, just seemed to happen because there was nothing else that could have happened. And if all Vera was trying to do the other night was point something out, then why hadn't she been able to be in the room with me since then? It seemed to me like she *hated* me now. Maybe it was childish of me to think my mother hated me, but I couldn't help it.

"First of all, Vera, Dustin and I just happened, it happened while we were rehearsing. So I haven't decided anything. And if you running from the room and slamming the door was you just pointing something out when I told you what had happened, then . . . then I don't know anything. You've been avoiding me; you haven't looked me in the eye; you've been practically living at Sam's since I told you. Didn't you think that I might need someone to talk to, that I might need you? It's not only Dad I miss, it's you too! Don't you miss me at all? Mom?"

I hadn't called Vera "Mom" to her face in years, and it sounded strange to do it. My emotions had gotten the better of me. I felt like she was being let off the hook just because she was an adult. I always thought of the two of us as best friends, as obnoxious as that sounds. I hadn't expected her to turn on me quite so easily.

"*Of course* I miss you, Blake. I'm so, so sorry," Vera exclaimed, rushing over to hug me. "It's just," she went on, "I don't have a problem with gayness, you know, Blake?"

"I never thought you did, not until the other night."

"When it's your own child," she continued, "it

seems different. It seems like a bigger deal. Maybe it shouldn't be. I know it shouldn't be, but, I'm surprised. And I really don't think anyone should be in a hurry to give himself a permanent label. Calling this a phase for you wasn't meant to make light of what's going on with your friend, with Dustin. It was my way of trying to make you feel like you had room to figure everything out in your own time. Because you were with Anna for a while, remember, Blake? And you liked her."

"I know Vera. I was, I did. But I like Dustin so much more than that. I feel differently about him; it seems more intense. Honestly I don't really know what's going on in any logical way. I only know how I feel."

Dad and Vera were quiet and eyed me curiously. I wasn't sure what they were going to say or do.

"You're honest, Blake. Which is in part why you're such a good actor, I expect. So . . . are you gonna tell us about Dustin? What's he like?" Vera asked, grinning.

I grinned too. As long as I felt like I was allowed to feel and think what I wanted to, I would be okay.

"How much time do you have?"

———

"How much time do you have? Dad? Before you guys have to hit the highway?"

Audrey, Dad, and I were all in the car driving toward Main Street to get breakfast. It was Sunday morning and their weekend in Eastport was coming to an end. I wanted to take them to Loretta's Market before they left.

"Only half an hour or so really, Blake. I wish we were staying longer. The Amtrak leaves Orono before noon."

We pulled into a parking spot right outside the market. It was early, only eight or so, and hardly anyone was out. The market had just opened up.

Dad and Audrey started to follow me toward the entrance but I quickly stopped them.

"No, no, you guys get us a spot by the picnic area. I'll get breakfast. It's on me."

"Well, thank you, Blake. That's so nice of you," Audrey called out to me as I ran inside the store.

I made a beeline straight for the bakery counter and ordered three large slices of cake to go. The autumn sunlight felt warm on my face as I ran down the steps and over toward the picnic table where Dad and Audrey were. They looked tired but happy. I felt the same way.

"Cake for breakfast, huh? Loretta was all out of coffee and toast this morning?" Dad joked as he eyed the cake suspiciously.

"She might as well have been," I answered, stuffing cake by the forkful into my mouth. "This is the best cake for miles around. You don't need coffee with this, Dad. The sugar alone will give you energy for a week."

"Wow!" Audrey exclaimed. "This is the best cake that I've ever had in my life."

I smiled. I was starting to like Audrey, no matter

how much I didn't want to. Things probably wouldn't change anytime soon either, so what good would it do to insist on hating her? It wasn't my decision who Dad lived with, it was his. Audrey seemed alright.

"Cliff would love this," she said to Dad.

"Who's Cliff?" I asked.

"My brother, the one I told you about on Friday—the cake fanatic. He's an entertainment lawyer; he's so much fun. Cliff lives in Seattle with his partner Tony. Tony owns a bakery out there too, the best in the city. You should come with us, Blake, when we visit them for New Year's. Their daughter Zara is adorable, too; here, I have photos I can show you."

Audrey dug through her bag to pull out her iPhone and started going through her photos. I looked from her to Dad in surprise.

"Your brother has a partner?"

"Yeah, that's right. Oh, here it is. I love this one, from when they went to Disney last month."

Audrey handed the phone to me, displaying a photo of a good-looking guy with red hair, who looked a lot like Audrey, holding a beautiful baby girl wearing Minnie Mouse ears. Standing next to them, with his arm around Cliff, was a gorgeous black guy who I assumed was Tony. I loved it.

"Audrey, why didn't you . . . I mean, why didn't you tell me on Friday, that your brother has a family and everything?"

She stuffed the last of her cake into her mouth.

"I didn't think it was a big deal. It's not really, not now. Sure, when we were in high school, when he first told me and our parents that he was into this guy Michael, it was a whole thing. But they got over it. It just kind of surprised us, I think, at the time. Because he'd had a few girlfriends before Michael, we just assumed he was straight. That's what I was trying to tell you on Friday night, Blake, that you don't have to worry so much about deciding something about yourself—deciding you're straight, deciding you're gay—and sticking to it.

You have to allow yourself to change your mind or to realize an alternative truth about yourself. It's your birthright, as a human being on planet Earth."

I stared at the photo of Cliff and his family again, then back at Audrey, who pushed her cleaned cake plate away in satisfaction. Dad was smiling at her and reached across the table to grab her hand. It reminded me of something else.

It reminded me of the way that Dustin looked at me. I made a mental note to thank him the next time that I saw him.

The familiar feeling of butterflies in my stomach, the palpable energy of the audience waiting for the scene to begin, the recognizable glint of excitement in Dustin's eyes . . .

It was Thursday afternoon and Troupe rehearsal had just begun when Mr. Perske and Ms. Miller made an announcement. They had decided that it would be a good idea if everyone shared their scenes from last rehearsal with the rest of Duncan High.

"It will be good performance practice for you!" Ms. Miller assured us.

"Besides, don't you want to share what you've

been working on with the rest of your classmates?" Mr. Perske asked us excitedly.

I looked around the gym. No one in the Troupe seemed too eager about the idea.

"Mr. Perske, don't you think it's a bit early to share with the rest of the school? I mean, we haven't had too many rehearsals yet," Marie said.

"Yeah, and don't we want them to be surprised when they come to the show? If we give it away now—" Niko added.

"Nonsense," assured Ms. Miller. "It's a preview of coming attractions. What better way than a *preview* to get the whole student body to come to the performances?"

I wasn't so sure. I couldn't imagine Schwartzman and his cronies sitting through our scenes without laughing or heckling. Neither could I imagine them coming to see the real performances when we had them.

"So," Mr. Perske went on, "go run through your scenes and work out the rough patches from last rehearsal. They don't have to be perfect, but do your best to get off-book."

Everyone stood up and went toward their rehearsal rooms.

"Ready, Blake?" I felt someone tap me on the shoulder.

It was Dustin. I felt relieved to see him and even more nervous than I had been last week. Maybe it was because I felt there was nothing holding me back now, nothing holding us back. Now that Vera, Dad, and Audrey knew about us, I couldn't think of a reason not to spend as much time with Dustin as possible.

"Yeah, ready. Think maybe we can top our last run-through?"

"It would be impossible not to," he answered, laughing. He was right about that.

I couldn't help laughing either. Suddenly it seemed so *ridiculous* how stressed out I had been about everything. Dustin and I liked each other a lot, and we were working on becoming better actors. Everything about what we were doing felt right and true.

"You seem extra happy today, Blake. Did you talk to your dad?" Dustin asked as he held the classroom door open for me.

"I certainly did, Dustin. And his wacky girlfriend Audrey, and Vera, my mom. It was an emotionally exhausting weekend. But I think it was good for everyone."

Dustin nodded and smiled. "That so?" he asked.

We put our stuff down and walked to our marks.

"And uh," Dustin went on, "whose idea was that, then? To have a bit of a *chat with your dad?*"

I smiled, glad to be with him again.

"I can't really remember. I assumed it was mine. No?"

Dustin raised an eyebrow at me.

"No. No it wasn't. My idea. You're welcome."

"Thank you, Dustin. Now say your line."

———

I could hardly stop my hands from shaking. This hadn't happened to me for a while, not since I had first auditioned for the Troupe. And this was a similar occasion, I supposed.

Ming was about to film me for our first YouTube series episode. She had been bugging me about it for so long, and now seemed like a good time to do it. I was on a high from the weekend with Dad and Audrey, and from having straightened things out with Vera, not to mention the possibility of what spending more time with Dustin might mean. I knew that whatever it was, it would probably be good. It would certainly coolify life in Eastport some, that was for sure.

"Are you ready, Blake? We should probably do a few test takes before we record it for the real deal."

Ming and I were in my room and she had set up her video camera tripod equipment. I had just gone through rehearsal with Dustin, which had gone really well, but this would be a monologue. It was Romeo's monologue, the famous one when he first sees Juliet— "But soft! What light through yonder window breaks?"—that one. I had worked on it here and there on my own but hadn't yet performed it in front of anyone.

"Sounds good, Ming. This thing, when you post it, better get at least one *million* hits from viewers in the first week. Deal?"

Ming rolled her eyes at me while she positioned herself with the tripod.

"Deal. Consider it done. Now will you get going? I have to go home and study for an Algebra exam after this," she said.

I cleared my throat, rolled my neck back and forth to relax myself, and closed my eyes for a moment. I tried to tap into the character of Romeo and all the actors who had played him at one point or another.

I opened my eyes to see the James Dean poster on the wall, and I tried to think of the scene that I'd loved recently in *East of Eden*. It was acting at its best and it was what I wanted to achieve.

"Okay, Ming," I said, taking a deep breath. I'm ready."

She gave me the three-two-one signal with her left hand and then motioned to me to start.

I hadn't gone through three lines when there was a knock at my bedroom door. We ignored it at first but when it continued, I cut the monologue short and told Ming to stop the recording.

"Blake? Sorry to bother you." It was Vera.

I had told her that Ming and I would be working up there, so I wasn't sure what she was doing.

"What's going on, Vera?"

She came into the room tentatively and spoke.

"Dustin's here. He says he wants to see you. Can I bring him in?"

I looked to see Dustin lingering behind Vera, his jacket still on, his hair wet with rain from outside. I wondered what he was doing here. Ming, still holding her camera, was practically swooning over him. He did look sort of irresistible.

"Hey, Dustin, what's . . . what's going on? We're

just working on some filming stuff, why don't you come in and check it out?"

He came in, smiling awkwardly. Vera gave us the once over, then left and closed the door behind her.

"Sorry for showing up out of the blue," Dustin said to me. "I was just on my way to pick up some groceries for my Mom, from Loretta's Market. She wanted coffee for tomorrow morning, which would have been fine, but I ran into Schwartzman on the way there."

He shook his hair out to dry it a bit and I noticed he seemed to be kind of shaken up.

"That idiot," Ming exclaimed. "What did he do?"

Dustin sighed and rubbed his face with his hands, flattening his wet hair down.

"Ah you know, the usual. Just called me a bunch of names. Most times it doesn't bother me. I mean, I know he's dumb. But this time there was this mom and her son packing their groceries up into their car. They heard Schwartzman shouting at me and laughing like a hyena. The mom gave me this look as she threw her kid into the car—like she was running away from a monster."

I hated to see him like this, so distraught and hurt and not himself. I could strangle Schwartzman.

But then I realized something. *There would always be Schwartzmans.*

"We can't fix the whole world, you know Dust? We can't cast a magic spell on Schwartzman and turn him into—"

"—*not an idiot?*" Ming interjected.

"Exactly. I bet every high school in the country has a Schwartzman. There will always be Schwartzmans. We have to, like, *not care.* You know?"

It was probably the smartest line I had said all day—that wasn't Shakespeare's, anyway. Ming watched Dustin as she readied her camera to reshoot my monologue.

Dustin walked to the window and stared at the nondescript scene outside.

"I'll try, Blake," he said quietly. "Hey, I can see the water from here, if I squint a bit and lean on one foot."

"Dust, come sit next to Ming for a minute. Maybe with a real audience, I can do a better job on this monologue," I said.

He sat next to Ming, who smiled at him. Shameless.

Just then there was another knock on my door.

"Come in!" I called, slightly exasperated. I was happy to see Dustin, but I was beginning to lose momentum here. The filming had been Ming's idea in the first place.

Vera came toward us with a huge plate of her chocolate chip cookies, which smelled freshly baked.

"Sorry to interrupt you guys, but I didn't want you to miss out on these," she said, placing the plate on the bed between Ming and Dustin.

"Wow, thanks Vera," Ming said, placing her camera to the side and grabbing a cookie.

"Hey," I called to her, "don't lose focus here, okay?"

"Okay," she answered me, with her mouth full.

"Hey, Vera," I said, suddenly getting an idea. "Why don't you stick around and watch my monologue?"

She smiled at me and sighed.

"I'd love to, Blake." Taking a seat next to Dustin, Vera reached for her iPhone in her pocket. "Do you mind if I call your dad and put him on video chat, so he can see too?"

"That's a great idea, Vera," I replied. Dad answered on the first ring.

"Hey Dad!" I shouted over in the direction of the phone. "Tell Audrey to come and watch, too!"

"She's right here with me, Blake. She's watching."

"Hey, Blake!" I heard Audrey shout.

"Hey, guys, so this is one of my monologues from the play. Ming and I are filming it to put on

YouTube and create a following of fans devoted to my acting career."

Ming raised an eyebrow at me, a sign for me to cool it with the ego stuff. I looked over at Dustin, who still seemed a bit shaken up but was trying to be a good sport nonetheless. I wanted to hug him and tell him that everything would be alright.

Ming pulled her move again, the three-two-one play from a few minutes earlier, queuing me in to start.

Maybe it was the fact that the people closest to me in my life were all in the same room watching, whether it was the poster of James Dean that stared me down as I performed, or whether it was the knowledge that the recording of this reading could potentially be viewed by thousands of people all over the world via the internet. But I felt really, really motivated, and tuned into the character and the whole play.

When I was done, Ming waited a second or two and then stopped the recording. Vera and Dustin sat there beaming and soon burst into applause. So did Dad and Audrey over the iPhone. It seemed like I had nailed it!

After we devoured the cookies, I saw Ming and Dustin to the front door.

"I'll send the video to you to check out, and then we can upload it, Blake. See you guys at school tomorrow."

She went off into the evening, and Dustin turned to look at me.

"Want to take a walk?" he asked.

"I'd love to," I replied.

He took my hand and we began a slow turn around my block.

"That was the best reading I've ever heard you give, Blake. We should blow the whole school out of the water at the performances."

"Thanks, Dustin."

His smile faded slightly from his face.

"The whole school minus Schwartzman, anyway" he said more quietly.

"Hey—there'll always be Schwartzmans, remember? I guess we just have to be really strong, you know? We can help each other do that," I said.

Dustin smiled at me and squeezed my hand. "You're right."

———

"Blake! Blake! Are you ready? You and Dustin are up next!"

It was the afternoon of the preview and the entire school was assembled on the other side of the makeshift stage curtain that Mr. Perske had set up in the gym. A few scenes had been performed so far, to raucous applause and cheers. The enthusiasm could've been because the entire school had gotten out of its third and fourth period classes to watch us perform. Nevertheless, I chose to believe it was mainly because the Troupe's rehearsing had paid off. I chose to believe it was because we were amazing.

I hoped that Dustin and I could do as well. He was a few feet away from me, pacing back and forth, reciting his lines to himself. I had never seen him this nervous before.

"Dustin, hey—Dust, you okay?"

He looked over sharply, like I had interrupted him. His eyes were wild.

"Dustin, do you have . . . *stage fright*?" I asked in disbelief.

"I haven't gotten it in a while, not since the sixth grade. It'll go away soon," he answered me, taking deep breaths.

"It'll be fine, okay? We can't possibly do any worse than when we performed it for the Troupe last time, right? And it's not the play, you know? It's just a preview—it doesn't have to be perfect," I told him, putting my hands on his shoulders to calm him down.

"I know, I . . . I know," he said.

Suddenly a roar of applause erupted from the audience, and Mr. Perske motioned for Dustin and me to head out on stage. I quickly grabbed Dustin's hand.

"Dust, remember—it's just us out there, okay? It's just me and you. Like it was in the rehearsal room. The audience makes no difference. Got it?"

He smiled at me and took a deep breath.

"Got it."

———

Whatever applause there had been for the scenes before us, there was twice that when Dustin and I finished our scene. It was the best we had ever performed it; our connection that had been there during our earliest rehearsals came back and was even amplified by recent personal events. I felt great.

Backstage, the rest of the Troupe, Ms. Miller, and Mr. Perske all congratulated us and patted us on the backs. It was the kind of response I had dreamed about my whole life, and I suddenly saw that it was not just a dream, but a real possibility. That I could live my life doing this kind of work and getting this kind of response and feeling this good. Maybe even on Broadway.

Dustin and I hugged; we knew that we had done well.

"Best ever, right?" I asked him.

"Best ever," he agreed. "Sorry I was kind of freaking out before."

"Don't apologize; I was nervous, too. The key is not to think about it. If I started to think about the audience too much, I'd never go out on stage."

After the preview was over, we all had to resume our normal class schedules of course. But it would be easy, still riding the high from Dustin's and my performance. The two of us couldn't stop smiling.

I walked Dustin to his next class and he was about to go in when Schwartzman showed up. Dustin's face grew red and angry. He'd probably had enough.

I was so sure that Schwartzman was going to

tease us about our scene. He had to have watched it, the whole school had attended. But somehow he seemed different; his eyes were wider and his overall energy less aggressive. Schwartzman averted his gaze and passed us right by in the hallway. No insults, jokes, shoves—nothing.

Dustin and I exchanged looks of confusion but chose to move on.

"I'll see ya later, Blake, yeah?" Dustin said as he reached his classroom.

"Sounds good to me. We should celebrate at Bernadette's. I'll text you."

As I walked to my classroom, Ming came running up behind me calling my name.

"Blake, you were so great!"

"Thanks, Ming."

"And your video—it just received its five-hundredth view on YouTube! Well, four-hundredth, if you subtract all the times I was trying to make sure it worked."

Wow, five hundred people—or four

hundred—had watched my monologue. Just some kid in the smallest, eastest of towns. Maybe I didn't need to rush for that Greyhound bus just yet.